ADDISON MOORE

Bobbing For Bodies

Murder in the Mix Mystery #2

ADDISON MOORE

Edited by Paige Maroney Smith
Cover Design: Lou Harper, Cover Affairs
Published by Hollis Thatcher Press, Ltd.

Copyright © 2018 by Addison Moore

This novel is a work of fiction. Any resemblance to peoples either living or deceased is purely coincidental. Names, places, and characters are figments of the author's imagination. The author holds all rights to this work. It is illegal to reproduce this novel without written expressed consent from the author herself.

All Rights Reserved.

Books by Addison Moore

Cozy Mystery

Cutie Pies and Deadly Lies (Murder in the Mix 1)
Bobbing for Bodies (Murder in the Mix 2)
Pumpkin Spice Sacrifice (Murder in the Mix 3)
Gingerbread and Deadly Dread (Murder in the Mix 4)

Mystery

Little Girl Lost

Romance

Just add Mistletoe

3:AM Kisses (3:AM Kisses 1)
Winter Kisses (3:AM Kisses 2)
Sugar Kisses (3:AM Kisses 3)
Whiskey Kisses (3:AM Kisses 4)
Rock Candy Kisses (3:AM Kisses 5)
Velvet Kisses (3:AM Kisses 6)
Wild Kisses (3:AM Kisses 7)
Country Kisses (3:AM Kisses 8)
Forbidden Kisses (3:AM Kisses 9)
Dirty Kisses (3:AM Kisses 10)

Stolen Kisses (3:AM Kisses 11)
Lucky Kisses (3:AM Kisses 12)
Tender Kisses (A 3:AM Kisses Novella)
Revenge Kisses (3:AM Kisses 14)
Red Hot Kisses (3:AM Kisses 15)
Reckless Kisses (3:AM Kisses 16)
Hot Honey Kisses (3:AM Kisses 17)

The Social Experiment (The Social Experiment 1)
Bitter Exes (The Social Experiment 2)
Chemical Attraction (The Social Experiment 3)

Low Down and Dirty (Low Down & Dirty 1)
Dirty Disaster (Low Down & Dirty 2)
Dirty Deeds Low (Down & Dirty 3)

Naughty by Nature

Beautiful Oblivion (Lake Loveless 1)
Beautiful Illusions (Lake Loveless 2)
Beautiful Elixir (Lake Loveless 3)
Beautiful Deception (Lake Loveless 4)

Someone to Love (Someone to Love 1)

Someone Like You (Someone to Love 2)
Someone For Me (Someone to Love 3)

Burning Through Gravity (Burning Through Gravity 1)
A Thousand Starry Nights (Burning Through Gravity 2)
Fire in an Amber Sky (Burning Through Gravity 3)

The Solitude of Passion

Celestra Forever After (Celestra Forever After 1)
The Dragon and the Rose (Celestra Forever After 2)
The Serpentine Butterfly (Celestra Forever After 3)
Crown of Ashes (Celestra Forever After 4)
Throne of Fire (Celestra Forever After 5)

Perfect Love (A Celestra Novella)

Young Adult Romance
Ethereal (Celestra Series Book 1)
Tremble (Celestra Series Book 2)
Burn (Celestra Series Book 3)
Wicked (Celestra Series Book 4)
Vex (Celestra Series Book 5)
Expel (Celestra Series Book 6)

Toxic Part One (Celestra Series Book 7)
Toxic Part Two (Celestra Series Book 8)
Elysian (Celestra Series Book 9)
Ethereal Knights (Celestra Knights)

Season of the Witch (A Celestra Novella)

Ephemeral (The Countenance Trilogy 1)
Evanescent (The Countenance Trilogy 2)
Entropy (The Countenance Trilogy 3)

Melt With You (A Totally '80s Romance)
Tainted Love (A Totally '80s Romance 2)
Hold Me Now (A Totally '80s Romance 3)

1

I see dead people.

It's true. I do see dead people on occasion, but it's mostly long-deceased pets that hop over from the other side to say hello—and, believe me, it's never a good sign for whoever they've come to greet. But, at the moment, I'm not looking at a ghastly phantasm. No, this is no ghost, and as much as I hate to admit it, she very much feels like a harbinger of ominous things to come.

The tiny metal newsstand that sits in front of the Honey Pot Diner has Merilee Simonson's face staring back at me from behind the glass. It was just last month that Honey Hollow had its very first homicide, and I was unlucky enough to discover the body. Merilee, my old landlord, was even unluckier to *be* the body.

I shake all thoughts of that hairy scary day out of my mind as I step out into the street to admire the newly minted bakery which Nell, my best friend's grandmother and my boss by proxy, has put me in charge of.

"The Cutie Pie Bakery and Cakery," I whisper as I take in the beauty of the divine little shop that I've gleefully been holing up in the last week solid while baking up a storm for today's grand opening. It's the beginning of October, and autumn is showing off all of its glory in our little corner of Vermont. Honey Hollow is famous for its majestic thickets of ruby maples, liquidambars, and bright yellow birch trees—all of the above with leaves in every color of the citrine rainbow. The sweet scent of cinnamon rolls baking, heady vanilla, and the thick scent of robust coffee permeate all of Main Street, incapacitating residents and tourists alike, forcing them to stagger down toward the bakery in a hypnotic state. I'm pretty sure I won't need business cards to pull in the masses. I'll opt for the olfactory takedown every single time. Not even the heavy fog that is rolling down the street this morning has the power to subdue those heavenly scents.

Hunter, my notorious ex-boyfriend's cousin, stretches to life as he stands from where he was crouching by the entry. Bear and Hunter have been working out in front for the last three days trying to repair cracks in the wall that divides this place from Nell's original restaurant, the Honey Pot Diner. Inside, a nice opening has been made in the south-facing wall so that patrons of both establishments can meander from place to place. And I'm glad about it, too. I've been a baker at the Honey Pot for so long I would have missed seeing the inner workings of it daily even though it is right next door. Not to mention the fact my best friend, Keelie, is the manager at the Honey Pot, so this guarantees I'll still see her smiling face each and every morning.

Hunter strides over and rests his elbow over my shoulder as we take in the sight together.

"Don't forget that part," he says, pointing to the smaller sign below the words I just read. "Fine confections, gourmet coffee, and more!" he reads it just as enthusiastically as the exclamation point suggests.

We share a little laugh, never taking our eyes off the place. Otis *Bear* Fisher—the aforementioned and somewhat infamous ex—and Hunter spent all last week getting the furniture for the bakery painted in every shade of pastel. Bear bought out all of the chairs and café tables he could find at his friend's chain of secondhand stores, and the end result is so sweet and cozy it's hard for me to leave this place at night.

"Thank you for all your hard work," I say, looking up at Bear's lookalike cousin. After Bear shattered my heart into shards as if it were a haunted mirror, it was Hunter who offered up his support and suggested I leave town for a bit to clear my head. I took his advice and hightailed it to New York—Columbia University to be exact—and, well, let's just say my heart was shattered ten times harder in the big city than it ever was in Honey Hollow. "You know, I've probably never said this before, but thank you for your friendship, too." I can't help but sniff back tears. "You really have been a rock in my life. I'm sorry I didn't get a chance to tell you sooner." I offer a quick embrace to the surly blonde with the body of a brick building. Both Bear and Hunter look as if they're primed to be lumberjacks with their tree-like muscles, but lucky for me their chosen profession just so happens to be construction.

"Whoa, easy, Lottie. Don't shed a single tear for me." He laughs at the thought. "I know this day is an emotional one for you. This bakery has been your destiny for as long as I can remember." He nods back to the place where his tools are strewn all over the sidewalk just under the scaffolding he's had set up for days to assist him in the exhausting effort. "Let me clean this mess up so you can get your party started." He jogs back to the sprawl of tools, and I quickly follow him under the canopy of this skeletal structure.

"It's not bad luck to stand under a scaffolding, is it?" I tease. I'll admit, my nerves are slightly jangled just thinking about the festivities about to ensue.

He barks out a short-lived laugh. "Nope, that would be a ladder. But you're not allowed to have any bad luck, period. This is your big day, Lottie Lemon, and I promise you not one thing will go wrong." He gives a playful wink, and something about that facial disclaimer sends me in a jittery panic ten times more than before. He winces. "I think I left something out back."

Hunter takes off, and no sooner does he leave than I press my hand to the window of the bakery, a no-no as far as Keelie is concerned. She's been helping me scrub and scour every inch of this place to get it ready for its big debut, but I'll gladly wipe away my own fingerprints in a moment just to garner one more look inside before we open. It's all there—the café tables and chairs look as sweet as confections themselves, the refrigerated shelves that line the front are fully stocked and loaded with every cookie, brownie, and delicious dessert you can think of, and the walls are painted a decadent shade of butter yellow. My sister, Lainey, came by yesterday to help me decorate the place for Halloween with ghosts, witches, and scarecrows set in every free space. Autumn leaves carefully line the counters, and tiny orange pumpkins dot each table with gold and red maple leaves blooming out from underneath them. To think that in just a few short hours this place will be filled with family and friends—with Everett and Noah. Noah who—

A horrible creaking sound comes from the scaffolding above me, and I look up in time to see the gargantuan structure rocking back and forth. My entire body freezes solid as it careens toward me, and before I know it, I'm hit from behind by a warm body, pushed to safety as the entire scaffolding crashes into a pile of dust. That metal newspaper stand is lying on its side, and Merilee's grinning face is staring back up at me in replicate.

"Oh my God," I pant as I struggle to catch my breath.

"Geez, lady." A man with dark curly hair, a lantern jaw, and eyes the color of espresso pats me down by the shoulders. "You okay? You almost got crushed to death." His eyes widen a notch at the thought as do mine.

"Yeah"—I glance down at my body, thankfully still intact—"I'm fine. You saved my life!" My hand clutches at the thought of me dying, right here in front of my own bakery on opening day of all occasions. How horrible that would have been for me and perhaps for all of Honey Hollow, considering there is a stockpile of sweet treats in there to feed the entire community for a month if need be. I'd hate to think that anyone would let all of my hard work go to waste just because I met an untimely demise, but I suppose seeing my body splattered like a dead fly might kill an appetite or two. "You have to come inside." I grip him by the sleeve, and he quickly frees himself with a shake of the head. "Please, let me give you a cake or something. You're a *hero*!"

"I'm no hero." He glances past my shoulder just as Hunter and Bear shout their way over. "I gotta run. I got a kid waiting for me at home." He jogs across the street and is swallowed up by the fog within two seconds.

"*Wait*," I call after him. "Please bring your family by later! We're having a party!"

"Lottie!" Bear pulls me in tight, and I struggle to breathe for a moment before inching away. "You could have been killed!" He turns his attention back to the carnage. "*Hunter*"—he barks—"how many times have I told you not to put heavy crap on top of the scaffolding?" he riots over at his cousin, and poor Hunter looks just as shaken as I do.

"I didn't. I swear." He kicks one of the hefty looking bags that almost crushed me right along with the planks on that scaffolding. "I'd never put bags of quick-set on there. I'm not that *insane*," he riots right back.

Keelie appears from nowhere and pulls me into the safety of the Cutie Pie Bakery.

"Don't you worry about a thing, girl." She slings her svelte arm around my shoulder as we take in this magical place, and somehow the trauma of what I've just been through begins to subside. "It's a good thing to get all of the bad luck out of the way up front." She bites down on a ruby red lip as if it isn't. Keelie and I bonded at an early age, and she's felt every bit like one of my sisters. Her blonde curls are pulled back into a ponytail, and her bright blue eyes glow as if someone lit a match behind them. Keelie is as peppy as she is sincere, and I love every attribute about her. "This is one of the best days of your life, and I never want you to forget a single moment of it. It's nothing but good luck from here on out."

"Right," I say, looking past my bubbly bestie, and with everything in me I want to believe her. "Nothing but good luck."

I glance back outside as Hunter and Bear work to clean up the debris. It's so windy those newspapers have come apart and are floating through the air like ghosts.

Then with a slap, the front page of one of those papers seals itself against the glass, and there she is, Merilee Simonson and her unnatural grimace looking right at me like a dark omen as if to say *there will be nothing good about this day.*

There is not one part of me that believes Keelie's kind words. There will be no good luck today.

Something tells me it will be bad, bad, bad.

2

Fall in Honey Hollow has always been a mainstay as far as the tourists are concerned, and seeing that it's early October I was expecting my fair share of leaf peeper foot traffic, but the number of bodies that have been passing through the Cutie Pie Bakery is enough to fill a cemetery.

I frown at my morbid analogy. I can't help it, though. After I nearly lost my life this morning when that scaffolding came down, I've been more than a bit shaken. I feel downright lucky to be alive and you'd think that thought alone would have me in a good mood, but there are cookies to be baked, cookies that are being *eaten* at a breakneck pace, thus the aforementioned hustle in the kitchen. Thankfully, both of the chefs from the Honey Pot, Margo and Mannon, have been helping out these past few days as we pump out batch after batch of delectable treats. The entire town holds the scent of vanilla and sugar at this point.

"Lottie!" Lainey comes at me with a death grip of a hug. Technically, we're not blood-related since the Lemons adopted me when I was just a few hours old, but Lainey and I have the same caramel-colored waves, same hazel green eyes. Even our features hold the same open appeal. Neither of us seems to go too long without offering the world a friendly smile. "I can't believe we pulled this off!" She takes a step back, and we admire the place together. Yes, it's Lainey's finishing Halloween touches that really make the bakery feel homey and well, a bit haunted. "Wasn't it a great idea to hang those witches by their pointy hats? I just love the way they're spinning over the refrigerated shelves!"

I glance to the stuffed witches as they twirl effortlessly in a circle. "They're great, and I love the pumpkins you brought in even more. They're adorable and really make it feel like fall." Lainey wanted to put up fake spider webs in every free corner, but since spider webs in general hold an unhygienic appeal, I opted out of that decorating disaster. I don't want the first impression of the Cutie Pie that the world sees to look as if I've never cleaned the place.

Keelie heads over with an empty tray and hands it to one of the many workers from the Honey Pot who is graciously helping me out today.

"We really need to get you a staff of your own. This grand opening is straining the Honey Pot. But don't you worry. I'm discerning just the right people to populate the bakery with." She leers over at me suggestively. "Guess who I saw pulling in across the street?" She bites down on a cherry red smile, a sure sign she's up to no good. "Everett and Noah just showed up."

"Together? In the same car?" I'm a bit stunned by this. I may have just met them both a few weeks back, but I know enough about their history to understand they're not the best of friends. They were stepbrothers for a time while they were both in high school, and it didn't end well between their parents—and, apparently, not between themselves either.

Keelie shrugs. "Who could tell. There are so many people out front, a spaceship could have dropped them off and I wouldn't have noticed." She gives a wild wave at someone coming in from the Honey Pot, and I look to find Keelie's grandmother, Nell, weaving her way over.

"Hello, girls!" She offers us both a spontaneous embrace. "How are two of my favorite granddaughters?"

She pinches my cheek with vigor. Nell is a sweet little ninety-two-year-old powerhouse who happens to own her fair share of real estate in Honey Hollow. The Honey Pot Diner and the Cutie Pie Bakery happen to be two of them.

"Fine and dandy." Keelie kicks my foot as she answers for me. "Should we tell her about the surprise?" She nods at her grandmother as if trying to get her to agree.

I glance to Lainey with wild eyes. Neither my sister nor I can fathom that life could get any better.

"What surprise?" I shoot Keelie an accusing glance. She knows I don't like surprises, and she knows I'm the last person on Earth I want anyone fussing over. The last time I got a surprise I was in a courthouse down in Ashford County when Everett took the stand as the judge presiding over the small claims court the Simonson sisters dragged me off to. Everett and I had just had a physical altercation of sorts, to put it delicately. We tripped and fell—and, well, I might have inadvertently used my head to hammer down over his crotch. It was not at all what you might think. It was totally accidental and not at all sexual even though his nickname Mr. Sexy was employed within the same hour. Everett *is* sexy, but then so is Noah. I let out a dreamy sigh just thinking about that man's lips. Noah's, not Everett's.

Nell clears her throat while shooting Keelie with venom herself. "It was going to be a true surprise if you hadn't said a word." She looks my way, and her features soften. "But, since the cat is halfway out of the bag, just know that I'll have to ask you to leave the shop a little early one night later this month, and when you get back in the morning, there will be something special waiting for you."

I gasp at the thought. "You are one naughty lady, Nell Sawyer." I elbow Keelie. "You're pretty naughty yourself. You know I don't need a single thing." I glance back at the gleaming stainless appliances—it was Noah who helped purchase them with the money his father stole from unsuspecting people, but I didn't know it at the time, and that marble island that sits in the middle of the kitchen was a surprise enough. I had ordered a simple counter constructed of stainless steel, but Nell canceled the order and had a beautiful stone island put in instead. Trays and trays of sandwich cookies, peanut butter bars, cream cheese swirled brownies, and chocolate macaroons sit upon it waiting to be brought out to the front for residents and tourists alike to enjoy. "Trust me, I already have everything, and if you continue to spoil me, I might just morph into a monster."

"You, a monster?" a deep voice strums from behind, and I'm greeted with a handsome Noah Corbin Fox looking just as vexingly good-looking as his surname suggests, and next to him stands Judge Essex Everett Baxter—who humbly goes by Everett. Noah is an intense man with a dangerous side that has a way of looking at me as if he were about to take me to the nearest bedroom and do amazing things to my body—all of which I wholeheartedly approve of. I've been in one serious sexual drought ever since the New York debacle, and Noah is just the right kind of trouble to alleviate me of all my frustrations.

Everett is dark and intimidating. He rarely, if ever, smiles, keeps his words to a minimum, and oozes testosterone to the point of demanding the attention of every female of every *species* to the forefront of his majesty.

"You're here!" I shout while throwing my arms around each of them at once. I hop back and take them in once again—Noah in a navy corduroy jacket and jeans, and Everett in his traditional three-piece inky dark suit. "Can you believe all of the people who are streaming through this place? I swear, it's all of Honey Hollow and then some have come to visit."

Noah takes in the crowd. Both Noah and Everett have the same dark hair, with the exception Everett's is jet-black and Noah's has a touch of red in the sunlight. Noah has the dreamiest marbled green eyes, and Everett's gaze is more of a blue heated flame. Both men are handsome in their own right, but it was Noah I took a bold step with a few weeks ago. We've been fused at the mouth pretty much ever since. And how I can't wait to fast-forward this day just to pull him into the walk-in like I did last night and shower him with all the affection I can. Who knew having a boyfriend could be such a stress reliever?

I touch my fingers to my lips a moment as if I had spoken those words out loud.

Noah and I aren't anything official. I shouldn't even be thinking the word *boyfriend* lest I accidentally pepper it in casual conversation. I'd hate to chase him off over some silly verbal blunder.

Noah winces. "I'd say you've got all of Vermont in here and part of New Hampshire, and Connecticut, too."

Everett chuckles at the thought. It still amuses me to see him smile. He wasn't at all friendly for at least the entire first month I knew him. It's a miracle we're friends at all.

"It's more like the Western Hemisphere." He nods to the feast out front. "I don't know about the rest of you, but I'm loading up."

Noah brushes a quick kiss to my cheek, and I can feel my skin heating to unsafe levels. Never have I had anyone show me physical affection in Honey Hollow before. Not even Bear, and we dated on and off for about three years in high school. I shudder just thinking about that time in my life.

"I'd better go with him." Noah frowns at this once-upon-a-stepbrother. "I'll make sure he leaves enough for the rest of us." He takes off after him just as I spot my mother circulating in the crowd, and I can't help but groan at the sight of her.

"She's here," I hiss to my sister.

Keelie bumps past us with a tray full of Honey Bars. "Don't sweat a thing!" she calls out as she heads to the front.

"I can't help it," I say, pulling my sister in close. "I don't trust this new guy Mom is dating."

Lainey scoffs. "You don't trust any guy Mom ever dates."

"I know that, but he's not culled from the usual bunch. The fact our mother is openly deviating from her usual pool of suspects makes me think that she might be serious about this guy." It's true. My mother has dated the same four men for as far back as the year after my father passed away. Oh, how I loved that man. And not just because he was the fireman who found me swaddled in a blanket on the cold floor of the firehouse. As much as I've struggled with abandonment issues sponsored by my birthmother, at least she didn't leave me in the woods to freeze to death. Joseph Lemon was a saint. I don't think I can say the same for the four clowns that my mother has switched out like a crop rotation since his untimely demise. But this new man, with his steely silver hair, his tall sturdy frame, his unyielding handsome features, he seems a lot more sinner than he ever does saint.

"Who cares?" Lainey's phone rings and she pulls it out of her purse. "Mom really likes this guy, and so should you. I've met him, and he seems pretty decent. You're going to love him." She holds out her phone, and my younger sister, Meg, waves manically our way on the other side of the screen.

"Congratulations, Lottie!" Meg laughs wildly as she looks past us into the room. "Can you believe it? All of your dreams have finally come true!" Meg looks a bit jarring with her harshly dyed jet-black hair teased every which way, and those signature yellow contact lenses of hers makes it feel as if Halloween were already upon us. "I gotta run, but eat some cookies for me, would you?" she roars menacingly into the screen, mostly to entertain us and quite possibly to get her in the mood for the rest of the night. Meg is a superstar on the Vegas female wrestling circuit. When she first started, Mom, Lainey, and I took a road trip to Nevada to see her in action. Seeing my little sister in that ring was the most frightening and yet empowering thing I have ever witnessed. Suffice it to say, Madge the Badge put on one heck of a show.

I spot Mom near the entry to the Honey Pot and glower at the man she has plastered to her side. Just as I'm about to bring up the boyfriend grievance to my sister's attention once again, a watery-eyed woman steps in front of me, and I blink a few times trying to process where I've seen her before.

"Micheline?" I take a half-step back just taking her in like this. I've known Micheline Roycroft for the better half of my life. She dated Hunter off and on while I dated Bear. I used to tease that we were clawing for the same life raft while on two different sinking ships. Her hair is longer, darker, her eyes a touch red and glossy, and she looks a bit forlorn. "My goodness, I've missed you!" I wrap my arms around my old friend. "Where have you been? Welcome to my new bakery!"

Her lips tremble with a smile. "I was living in Hollyhock for a while, working at the bank. I just transferred to Honey Hollow Savings and Loans. I moved back about a month ago." She gives a side-eye to the crowd. "Have you seen Hunter? I thought he'd be here since he helped with the construction."

"Oh, he's here somewhere. Are you two trying to work things out again?" I'm almost sorry I asked, considering the fact she seems on the verge of tears.

Micheline cranes her neck into the crowd and mumbles something about *later* before threading herself into the thicket of bodies.

Mom dances her way over with open arms. "Here you are!" She offers a firm embrace before pulling forward the man of the hour—more to the point, the man of my discontent. "Wallace, this is my middle daughter, Lottie. It's her special day, and I can't believe I'm alive and breathing to witness it!"

"Gee, thanks for the depressing endorsement. It's nice to know you believed in me so strongly."

She swats me. "You know I do."

It's true. I do.

Her gentleman caller extends his hand, and I can't help but frown at the over-sized mitt before I give it a shake. "Wallace Chad." His voice is warm and deep, and yet despite the equally warm twinkle in his eyes, I can't help but distrust him. "My pleasure to finally meet you. You have an amazing mother, as you both know." He nods a quick hello to Lainey.

Mom lifts a finger as if a thought just came to her. "Lainey, I've been meaning to tell you to make sure that garage of yours is locked up tight at all hours of the day. We heard Becca Turner just tell a crowd in the Honey Pot they've had a rash of burglaries right here in Honey Hollow." She taps her fingers over her lips as if the thought were unspeakable, and it is. That homicide we had last month was pretty unspeakable, too. It's just too much to wrap my head around. My heart still bleeds for Merilee.

Mom tugs at her new beau's lapel. "We'd better work the room. I'd hate for my friends to miss the opportunity to meet one of the kindest men on the planet."

Wallace leans toward Lainey and me. "I'm a financial planner by trade, so if there's anything I can ever do for you, it would be my pleasure to be at your service. Free of charge, of course."

Mom squeals as if we just won the lottery. "*Free!*" she shrills, making crazy eyes at both Lainey and me. "Isn't that something? You never get anything free these days." She looks to her silver fox of a boy toy. "Now you're just far too generous to me."

"Only because I can't begin to repay how generous you've been to me."

They blend back into the crowd, and I turn to Lainey and gag.

"I don't even want to think about how generous our mother is being. If you'll excuse me, I need to check the ovens and make sure nothing's burning. God knows I've been a little distracted today."

I take off for the back, and the scent of fresh devil's food cupcakes cooling on the rack has me swooning. Those delectable delights have been flying off the shelves—or trays as it were, so I've been baking them nonstop. It was Nell's idea to have an all-you-can-eat dessert bar. She said that would be a surefire way to get everyone addicted to my tasty treats, and when the shop officially opens for business tomorrow, I'll have a line out the door. She was also gracious enough to pay for all of the ingredients I'd need to pull off a feat such as this.

Lord knows I wouldn't be anywhere without Nell in my life. She's the one who gifted me my precious cat, Pancake. She happens to own Pancake's brother, Waffles, and our shared affection for the adorable, yet severely aloof,

Himalayans is just another facet of our inextricable bond. I'm pretty bonded to Pancake, too. In fact, I'm going to collapse on my bed with my arms wrapped tight around him tonight.

Technically, it's not my bed. I'm still holed up in Lainey's guest room, but once I get a little time on my hands, I'll be back to apartment hunting so I can get out of her hair. We get along well enough, but we've never made good roommates.

The back door is open, and I meander over for a quick breath of crisp autumn air. The fog is still rolling in thick, unfurling like batting, and I'm momentarily drawn to it. No sooner do I get to the back porch than I'm stopped in my tracks by the sound of shouting voices escalating to my left. Not far off in the alley, I spot Bear and Hunter going at it, both men red-faced and angry. It looks pretty volatile, so I quickly step back into the shop. I know for a fact Bear blamed Hunter for that scaffolding incident this morning, but I wish he wouldn't hammer into him like that. It was an accident, and everybody involved survived.

I head back into the bakery, picking up a tray of creamy white cake pops swirled to look like mummies, complete with chocolate chip eyes. The kids especially love those and, sure enough, every last one of them is snatched from me before I have a chance to set the tray down.

Everett comes up and bumps his shoulder to mine as we inspect the wild crowd. "That went fast. But then, so is everything else. Bear's brownie bar is a pretty big hit, too."

"Don't I know it. At least I can count on the fact they'll love my brownies." It was in honor of Bear that I put up the brownie bar to begin with. It turns out, he put this project at the top of his construction roster just so he could complete it as soon as possible.

"They'll love everything," Everett assures before nodding to the entry that leads into the Honey Pot, and I hike up on my tiptoes to see what he's motioning to.

I suck in a quick breath at the sight of Cascade Montgomery, Merilee and Mora Anne's cousin. And here I thought she was the one who stabbed poor Merilee in the back, but actually it was her sister, Mora Anne.

"Well, I'm glad she's here. Actually, I'm glad everyone's here."

I take in the crowd again and spot Holland Grand, who owns the orchard, speaking with Ken and Molly McMurry, who own the pumpkin patch. Next to them stands Naomi Turner, Keelie's twin sister. But, unlike Keelie, Naomi has decided to eschew her naturally blonde locks and dye them a gorgeous shade of ebony much like my own sister. Her eyes are a startling shade of blue, and I must admit the combination looks stunning. Both Naomi and Keelie are stunning in general. Next to her stand her best friend, Lily Swanson, and her newly minted beau, Travis Darren. I can't help but scowl over at him since he was dating both Simonson sisters at the very same time just last month.

Past them stand Becca Turner, aka my second mom, Naomi and Keelie's mother, speaking with Eva Hollister, the woman who runs my mother's book club, and Chrissy Nash, the mayor's ex-wife. And seeing that Mayor Nash himself is here mingling amongst the crowd, I'd say Chrissy is finally past the point where she can't stand to be in the same room with him.

To their left, Collette Jenner postures for the attention of every male in a three-mile radius. Apparently, she's one of Everett's many exes, and I can't help but grunt at the sight of her. Sure, she's a perky redhead who makes it a point to brighten any room she's in with that obnoxious witch-like cackle, but there's something about the fact Everett used to date her that has made me unsure of how I feel about her anymore. It's not like we were friends to begin with.

Just as I'm about to tempt Everett with one of my wickedly delicious devil's food cupcakes, something small and furry scurries across the floor, and I gasp as if trying to suck all of the oxygen out of the room.

"A *rodent*," I hiss to Everett, suddenly regretful I said anything at all. God forbid word get out that I've got rats or bats or whatever that thing was that just skipped into the place.

"What? Where?" Everett looks to the ground right along with me.

The tip of a fluffy little tail threads through the crowd, and my jaw unhinges. "It's not a rat after all. It's a squirrel." I'm only a touch relieved by that fact. It's still a menacing rodent, *vermin* if you will. And I certainly don't care to have it in my shop. I would have said all of that out loud, but I'm terrified of starting a stampede for the front door.

"I don't see it."

"It's right there." I point as the brazen little beast comes forward and stands on its hind legs right in front of my mother. Dear God, she's going to stomp it to death with those four inch stilettos she's stuffed her feet into. My mother is notorious for stomping out the life of a vermin or two, mostly mice and rats that found their way far too close to her killer clogs. She would do anything to defend her daughters, and a spontaneous homicide has never been off the table.

"Right where?" Everett leans in toward the spot my finger is poised to.

"Are you blind?" I tease as the creature takes a few ambling steps in our direction, and I freeze solid. That silver bushy tail, that fuzzy gray coat is suddenly translucent in nature, and I can see the floor right through its body. This isn't your run-of-the-mill woodland creature. This was once somebody's loveable, and well past its prime, pet.

"I'm beginning to question your vision." Everett looks stymied by what it is I'm staring at.

"Oh"—seeing that this beast is for my eyes only, I think it's best I ditch this entire conversation with him—"you're right." My cheeks flush pink as I stand straight as a pin. "It must have been a scarf someone dropped momentarily. It's about freezing outside already." A thought occurs to me, and I jolt to attention.

Dear God! The last time I saw a dearly departed beast it was Merilee's orange tabby and look what happened to her! Merilee, not the tabby. The pets that skip over from the other side of the rainbow bridge are *always* a prequel to some horrible event in their previous owner's life. The trouble used to range from skinned knees to broken bones, but in Merilee's case, that cat might as well have been dressed like the Grim Reaper. I've seen the ghost of a person just twice before, as well, and I'm darn glad I haven't seen one since. The squirrel comes up and holds its tiny paws up in my direction, just looking at me with those big brown eyes, that bushy tail hiked at attention, and I can't help but coo at it.

"Oh my goodness, you are the sweetest little thing," I whisper as I give it a quick scratch over the back.

"Lottie?" Everett sounds more than worried for me.

I straighten once again as the tiny creature scuttles past me, making his way to the kitchen.

Everett's dark brows bounce with concern. "Are you feeling okay? Who were you talking to?"

"You!" My voice squeaks. "I was talking to you. You're just the sweetest thing." I bite down hard over my lower lip. Lying is something I'm loath to do. "Say! If anyone in this room were to once have had a squirrel as a pet, who would you think that would be?"

"*Me.*" A warm, masculine voice buzzes in my ear as Noah wraps his arms around me, and my heart lurches inside my chest.

"Please tell me you're kidding," I say, spinning around in his arms to take in his gorgeous face. I couldn't stand it if anything even remotely bad happened to Noah. My heart hurts just thinking about it.

That tick of his cheek spells out concern. "I am kidding." He opens his mouth to say something else just as the McMurrys come upon us.

Molly smiles at both Noah and me. "I hope we're not interrupting." My eyes flit to that shoulder-length bob of hers with its cute, vertical curls. I've been envious of everyone who can pull off that hairstyle. I've wanted to try it myself this summer, but I never had a free moment. And now with the bakery, I'm afraid my hair will be set in a messy bun permanently. Her husband, Ken, is classically tall, dark, and handsome. He always has a toothy grin at the ready and a piece of straw tucked behind his ear that gives him a scarecrow-esque appeal.

"Not interrupting at all," I say, fully relieved to steer all conversation away from that poor deceased squirrel.

"Good," Molly says, holding up a purple frosted devil's food cupcake with a tiny meringue ghost spiked into the top. "Ken and I were wondering if you'd be up for baking about twelve dozen or so of these for the Fall-O-Ween Fest down at the pumpkin patch? Of course, we'll pay you and be happy to do it. Each year we like to offer a refreshment table, and these would be a perfect treat to go along with it."

"*Yes*! Of course, I would." A rush of adrenaline bursts through me all at once. "I would love to furnish any and all of the treats you need for the Fall-O-Ween Fest. It happens to be one of my fondest memories growing up."

"That's perfect." Molly's entire face brightens as if my cupcakes had the power to make her day, and I'd like to think they did. "I'll get you a firm number of how many we'll need, then email me with an estimate of the cost, and I'll come by next week and leave a deposit."

"I sure will," I say as they weave their way back into the crowd. Collette crops up in their place and immediately begins asking Everett ridiculous questions in a clear effort to pry him away.

I look to Noah. "I'll be right back. I'd better refill those cupcakes so that Molly and Ken can see firsthand how much the locals love them."

Noah ticks his head toward Nell. "Sounds good. I'll head over and say hello."

I take off for the kitchen, and just as I'm about to steal a fresh chocolate chip cookie off a cooling rack and pop it into my mouth—there is nothing like a warm chocolate chip cookie straight from the oven—that bushy silver tail garners my attention once again.

A horrible feeling of foreboding comes over me as I follow the wily beast as he makes his way out the back door. Carefully, I take a step out into the chilled autumn air. The maples from across the way have blown their golden hand-shaped leaves all over the ground as the tiny squirrel scampers over them and right over a body.

A scream gets locked in my throat.

Flat on his back lies Hunter Fisher with one of my devil's food cupcakes in his hand and a bullet wound through his chest.

Hunter isn't ever going to finish that cupcake. In fact, he won't be eating anything at all ever again.

He's dead.

3

The echo of my own screams riots through the tiny alleyway as a crowd amasses from nowhere, and soon it seems as if the entire bakery has drained of all its patrons to gawk at poor Hunter who lies motionless, his eyes still opened to the sky. Judging by that sizable pool of blood beneath him, Hunter Fisher is most certainly no longer with us.

Noah grabs ahold of me and pulls me back while Everett shouts into his phone for help to arrive.

"Lottie, what happened?" Noah weaves us through the tangle of bodies, and I can finally catch my breath. "What did you see?"

The crowd whispers Hunter Fisher's name until it sounds like an ominous chant.

"I didn't see any—" That squirrel! "Well, I guess that mystery is solved," I say under my breath. It's clear the adorable creature belonged to Hunter at some point in time.

Noah runs his hands up and down my arms as I startle back to life. "You saw something. What did you see?"

Everett comes up before I can answer. "The sheriffs are on their way. They want you to stick around for questioning."

"Sadly, I know the routine," I say as Bear comes running out of the back of the bakery just as a fire truck rolls onto the scene.

"What's going on?" He pushes his way through the crowd. "Oh God!" He dives onto his knees toward his poor cousin lying helpless on the asphalt, and I barrel through the knot of bodies to be with him.

"Who the hell did this?" The veins in the sides of his neck distend like cords as his face turns an instant shade of red. I've never seen him so filled with rage and grief.

I fall next to him, and Bear lets out a mighty roar as if he had some primal capability to morph into the beast from which his nickname was hewn. Bear loses it, cussing and shouting at anyone and everyone before leaning over his lookalike. Poor Bear just sits there stunned, red-faced and angry as if he were ready to kill whoever was responsible for this. And I have no doubt he would. If I never knew it before, Bear loved Hunter like a brother.

Before long, sirens saw through the air, and the dim alleyway is lit up with spasming red and blue lights. Most of the crowd has dissipated, and as soon as Captain Turner gets out of his vehicle, he instructs anybody who didn't witness the event to please leave their names with the attending officers before they head home. Not long after, an all too familiar coroner's van pulls up behind the brigade of patrol cars, and my blood runs cold.

It's happening again. It's already happened.

Captain Turner helps Bear up and pulls him to the side for questioning, and it's just me staring at my old friend as tears of my own stream down my cheeks.

"It's not fair," I say to no one in particular.

Noah materializes from out of nowhere. "You're right, Lottie. It's not fair. Murder never is." He helps me to my feet and holds me as I do my best to pull it together, but I can't seem to stop shaking, can't stop the tears from streaming like a wild river with no end and no beginning.

Keelie and Lainey head this way, shaken and pale themselves.

"Here," Lainey says while dabbing my cheeks with a wad of tissues. "I'm going to get you home. Captain Turner knows that you're staying with me. You shouldn't be here, seeing him like this."

"No." It comes from me like an abrupt protest. "I need to be here. I need to be here for Hunter and for Bear. You go ahead." I spot Tanner Redwood behind her and can't help but frown. It shouldn't be Tanner making sure my sister gets home safe. It should be Forest Donovan. Forest and Lainey were high school sweethearts who dated for a small eternity. But then, they hit a bump in the road last summer, a boulder if you will, and, well, Lainey thought it would be cute to make Forest jealous with Tanner. One date led to another, and they've been joined at the hip ever since. Not literally. And as far as I know, ever. Just the thought makes me want to gag.

Just as Lainey is about to protest, Forest comes over all decked out in his firemen garb, heavy yellow coat, loose tan pants, and thick black boots. Forest is every bit the hot firefighter with his chestnut waves and those crystal gray eyes.

Tanner looks more like your typical playboy—which everyone knows he is. My sister is so fooling herself if she thinks he's being loyal to her. I spotted him speaking to three different girls just this week alone. He happens to be the head of Parks and Recs for all of Honey Hollow. He's got a tanned surfer look about him, hair that's short in the back and longer in front so he's forever doing that annoying head flip to get it out of his eyes.

"Lainey"—Forest offers her a partial embrace—"thank God you guys are okay. When I heard it was the new bakery—" His voice breaks, and he ticks his head to the side as if working hard to keep his emotions in check. "Let me take you home."

Her mouth opens as she looks to Tanner.

"Dude." Tanner gently removes Forest's hold on my sister, and my heart breaks for my sister's one true love. That would be Forest, by the way. "I'm taking her home." He does that annoying hair flip thing three times in a row, and I'm starting to think it's a tic. "And I'll stay with her all night long."

"No thank you," I'm quick to interject, and my sister makes wild eyes at me as if to say thank you herself. "I'll be home as soon as I can, and I'll take over from there."

The three of them say a quick goodnight as Lainey and Tanner take off in one direction and poor Forest in the other.

Everett gives my shoulder a quick squeeze. "Are you okay? Did you see anyone taking off when you came out here?"

Noah's chest puffs up on cue. "I already asked her that. What did you see, Lottie? Did you hear anything?"

"No." I shake my head, bewildered. "I mean, he was shot, right? I certainly didn't hear a gunshot."

Noah nods. "They most likely used a silencer. Did you see anything at all? Anything?"

"No, I mean, yes. I was just following that sq—" My fingers land hard over my lips, and I shoot a quick look to Everett.

"Detective Fox," Captain Turner shouts as he motions him over.

Noah looks from me to Everett. "I'll be right back. Don't go anywhere."

Everett wastes no time leaning in. "You were going to say squirrel, Lemon. Don't deny it. We may not be in a courtroom, but I don't think it would be beneficial for you to perjure yourself in my presence regardless."

"Please." I avert my gaze a moment. "I would never lie to you—willingly." I wince as that last part comes out. "Besides, it's not important. What's important is that they catch whoever did this. And I can promise you, Essex Everett Baxter, that it was not me," I hiss out that last part, and to my surprise a tiny smile twitches on his lips. "*What?*" It comes out annoyed, as has been my go-to emotion with him in the not-so-distant past.

He straightens a bit, and his jaw squares out, making him look irritatingly far more handsome than ever is fair. Which reminds me—I know firsthand they label his java cup *Mr. Sexy* down at the coffee shop next to the courthouse. "You're not telling the truth."

A breath hitches in my throat. "How dare you insinuate that I'm a liar."

He leans in with those serious eyes. "I never called you such thing. I just so happen to be very good at reading people—and I have my ways of getting information out of just about anyone. It's my gift." His brows twitch. "You saw that squirrel again, didn't you?"

My hand clamps over my mouth, and I hop back a step in the event I need to bolt from this human lie detector machine. There's no way I'm telling Everett about my gift—or curse as it were. And at this point, I think it's a little too late to convince him that there was a real squirrel in question. The best thing to do is drop it.

Noah heads over and wraps his arms around me, dotting a gentle kiss over my forehead, and I take in his spiced cologne, allowing myself to relax over his rock-hard chest. I'm so exhausted from everything that's transpired tonight—this entire last week. The nonstop baking alone is enough to make anyone delusional. I'm hoping I'll wake up tomorrow morning to find my sweet cat Pancake curled up in my arms, and this will have all been one long nightmare.

Noah gently lifts my chin with his finger. "Captain Turner wants us to speak with him."

No sooner do I look over than Jack, Captain Turner as he's known to everyone else, is upon us. Jack is Keelie's dad, and since I've grown up with him as a second father, I've only ever called him by his proper name. Next to him stands a tall woman in a dark pantsuit. Long amber hair parted straight down the middle hangs over her shoulders. Her face is pale and offset morbidly by dark crimson lipstick. On anyone else it would look like a disaster, but she looks every bit the supermodel and pulls it off effortlessly.

Jack nods to me. "Lottie, this is Detective Ivy Fairbanks. She'll be asking you a few questions." Someone calls for him from behind, and he gives a quick bow. "I'll be right over here if you need me."

"Detective Fairbanks." Noah extends his hand, and she glares at it as if it were a rodent. Noah drops his hand. "My name is Noah Fox. I'm a private investigator myself, licensed in the state of Vermont."

She gives him a quick once-over. "Did you find the body?"

Noah turns to me. "No, actually—"

"Then you're dismissed." She tips her nose toward Everett and me. "Which one of you found the body?"

I clear my throat. "That would be me. And if you don't mind, I'd prefer we address him by his name, Hunter." My gut wrenches just hearing his name sail from my lips. "He was my friend."

"Very well." She pulls out a notebook, looking perennially bored. "What happened?"

I quickly relay the chain of events, sans any mention of Hunter's pet squirrel. For a moment, I wonder what Hunter had named him. He was so cute and fluffy. It was obvious anyone could have fallen in love with the tiny creature. I bet it was something cute and clever like Acorn. Hunter always did have a soft heart.

"So, that's it?" She blinks up at me with those dark coffee-colored eyes, and a chill runs through me. Sure, she's beautiful, but she's equally intimidating, and it has nothing to do with her beauty.

"That's it."

"You were just coming out for some air?" She glowers over at me. "With a bakery full of people and six batches of cookies in the oven? Hmm." Her lips crimp into something that looks like a smile while she simultaneously stares me down. It's an unnerving feat, and coming from her, it feels like a mental interrogation. "I'll be speaking to you again soon. Hopefully, something else will come to mind."

Noah wraps his arm around me. "I'll try to jog her memory. If anything new crops up, I'll let you know as soon as possible."

Detective Fairbanks straightens a moment, looking at him as if he were a vagrant who wandered onto the scene. "Have the Fishers hired you for your services?" There's a mocking undertone in her voice, and instantly I don't appreciate it or her.

A breath expires from him as he relaxes against me with an air of defeat. "No, they haven't."

"Then stay out of my investigation." She stalks off, and my jaw roots to the ground.

"How dare she speak to you that way," I say as I give his chest a light scratch. "I'm going to have her fired."

A deep rumble of laugh lives and dies in his throat as his eyes sparkle my way.

"Don't worry about her. She doesn't have the power to slow me down." He glances to our left a moment. "Hang tight. I'm going to talk to Bear and see what I can glean."

Everett pops up just as Noah takes off. "Now that we're alone, I think you owe me an explanation regarding that squirrel you claim to be chasing."

An incredulous laugh strums from me. "I owe you no such thing, Judge Baxter. Like I said, it was nothing."

Everett folds his arms across his enormous chest, his suit drawing tight around his elbows. "It was something, Lemon. And if you don't tell me, you'll have to tell Noah or Detective Fairbanks. Like it or not, whatever you saw led you straight to the scene of a homicide. You don't want to be guilty of withholding evidence, do you?" His tone drops several octaves when he says that last part, and you would think he were fifty years older than me rather than simply half a decade.

"Withholding evidence?" I practically mouth the words.

"That's right. People get sent to prison for it all the time."

A dull laugh expels from me in a powder white plume. But Everett isn't laughing. He's dead serious.

"Prison." I gulp at the thought of being forced to wear orange for years at a time. That alone sounds like a punishment. "Everett"—I plead with him—"I can't—"

"You can and you will," he says it stern, and a moment of thick silence bounces between us. "Fine. If you don't tell Noah or Detective Fairbanks by the time the night is through, I'm afraid I'll have to bring this information to light. I hope you don't take offense to it. It's simply my civic duty. My duty for justice doesn't end when I leave the bench."

My heart strums wildly in my chest. My entire body slaps with heat from embarrassment. I can't imagine me ever telling Everett something that sounds so insane. Something that *is* so insane.

My mouth opens and not a sound comes out. I glance over to Noah as he's comforting Bear, and my heart aches for the both of them. For Bear because he lost someone he loved like a brother. And for Noah because he's about to wish he never met someone as certifiable as myself.

"Hey"—Everett leans in with heavy concern in his eyes—"I don't want to upset you any more than you already are. I can see this is hard for you."

"Oh? Because you're good at *reading* people?" I can't help but smear it with sarcasm.

"Yes." He frowns. "Okay, here's the deal. You don't have to tell Noah or Detective Fairbanks for now. I'll come by the bakery some time this week, and you can fill me in once you've had a moment to relax. I wouldn't pry so hard unless I thought it was important. A man died, Lemon. Believe me when I say even the smallest shred of evidence can help put away whoever did this."

"Fine." I swallow hard, trying to push the next words out. "I'll tell you. Sometime this week." Maybe.

"You will." Everett looks every bit as intimidating if not more than Detective Fairbanks could ever hope to be. "And, Lemon?" he says as Noah heads back in this direction. "I'll know if you're not telling the truth."

"Yes, sir, Judge Baxter." I look up at him sternly from underneath my lashes. "I promise to tell the truth and nothing but the truth." I'm not crossing my fingers. I'm crossing my *soul*. I hope to God I don't accidentally spew the truth his way at any point during this next week or ever.

"Good. I'm counting on it."

We look back at the crime scene just as the area is cordoned off with caution tape, a blinding shade of yellow in this dim light. A photographer circles poor Hunter as men with plastic gloves begin to comb every inch of the alleyway.

I will tell Everett the truth.

Just as soon as I come up with some other truth to tell.

Poor Hunter is dead. And I'm more than positive that feral, long-dead creature won't add anything worthwhile to the investigation.

There's not a ghost of a chance.

4

Honey Hollow is robed in fog this early Monday morning. All of Main Street is blanketed in cardinal maple leaves, a red carpet fit for royalty, and yet here we are, grounded common folk blessed with the honor. It might still be early in October, but the Halloween spirit is alive and well with every last nook and cranny of this tiny town dotted with bright orange pumpkins in every shape and size. Just down the street in the town square, there's a heap of pumpkins surrounding Honey Hollow's enormous three-tiered stone fountain, and just beyond that, Founders Square Park has a friendly looking scarecrow staked at the entry that every tourist stops by to take their picture with. That's the thing that I have always appreciated about Honey Hollow. It's a warm, comfortably cozy small town that makes any and everyone feel right at home. I used to add that it was safe—that I felt much safer here than in the big city, but after everything that's transpired, I'm not so sure about that.

The day wears on, and I've been at the bakery now for hours. I've made it a practice to show up at five in the morning just to get everything started. Keelie said she'd help me hire my own staff since most of the staff working alongside me is on loan from the Honey Pot.

Margo and Mannon, the chefs next door, have been a godsend, utilizing their five-star superpowers to help streamline my baking and create a few marvels of their own in the process. I just finished with three dozen hazelnut bars, a dozen cutie pies, the famous, or perhaps infamous caramel apple treats that were served at the Apple Festival last month. I've filled the cupcake shelves with red velvet, French vanilla, and a devil's food variety frosted in colors of green, purple, and orange, each with either a black tarantula made from licorice, a meringue ghost, or a tiny chocolate cookie cut out in the shape of a wizard's hat, complete with candy stars. I kept the sign for Bear's Brownie Bar and moved it into the casing where I have a variety of brownies and blondies to choose from. I made up an entire tray of cheese and raspberry Danishes, along with fresh croissants for the morning crowd, in addition to a couple loaves of crumb cake.

When Keelie helped me order the coffee equipment for the bakery, I nearly passed out at the expense, but she promised it would be worth every robust drop, and once I learned to navigate my way around the steely beasts—and more to the point, now that I consider us friends, that beast is producing something magical that I never thought coffee could be. Suffice it to say, the bakery smells divine. I have no doubt the scent of rich, roasted java beans, coupled with the scent of fresh pastry dough baking has thoroughly permeated Main Street. I had the cinnamon rolls in the oven at about seven when we opened, and that's what truly brought in the heavy morning rush. But now that most of the crowd has dissipated and my molasses spice cookies and pumpkin cheesecakes are still in the oven, I've decided to pull my laptop out and sit in the café among the customers while my poor, tired feet do their best to recoup.

The bell on the door rings and in comes Lainey along with another small crowd. One of the girls from the Honey Pot motions for me to stay put while she takes their order.

"Hey, hey!" Lainey takes a seat across from me. "How are you doing? I'm surprised you're here. I thought for sure you would have at least taken a day off after last night." She ticks her head toward the back where Hunter's body was found.

"It's my official first day." I make a face at the thought because yesterday felt far more official. "And there are no days off when you're running the show. Nell expects me to be here. This is my baby as much as it is hers, and I'm going to make sure it succeeds."

Lainey waves me off. "That's a given. But you need to take care of yourself, too, lady." She peers over at my laptop. "Whatcha looking at? You weren't serious about setting up a kitty cam, were you? Because if my house is going to be under surveillance, I want to know about it. The last thing I want you to see is me dancing around in my leopard print robe. It's short, you know."

"Oh, I know it is." I avert my eyes at the memory of it. "Which reminds me. I know what to get you for Christmas. The rest of that robe."

"Ha-ha." She scowls as she leans in further. "What is this? Online classified? The real estate section?" Her voice pitches with the epiphany. "You're not thinking about moving out so soon, are you?" Lainey whines in that adorable way only she can. My sister looks every bit the Kewpie doll with her bowtie lips and perfectly coifed curls. She's head to toe in eggplant today, wearing a deep purple dress with a matching cardigan. Lainey always makes it a point to dress up for work. Nobody loves working at the library as much as my sister. Books are her passion as much as baking is mine.

The bell rings behind us again and in strides Noah Fox clad in a suit, that naughty smile twitching on his lips just for me, and my stomach bisects with heat at the sight of him.

"Hello, ladies."

Lainey pulls up a seat for him. "Please talk my sister out of looking for a place of her own. She's hardly home as it is. Paying rent wouldn't make sense at this point."

I can't help but shoot my sister a disparaging look. She's right, and I happen to hate when that happens, especially when I'm disagreeing with her.

"You looking for a place?" Noah spins his seat around and sits on it backwards, and something about that boyish move tugs at my heart.

"Yes," I say it low as if Lainey couldn't hear. "And you look extremely dapper and handsome, might I add." I can't help but bite down a naughty smile of my own. "Where are you off to today?"

"The office for now." He ticks his head in the direction of the bank. Noah's office is right next door to that financial institution. Actually, that's how we met. I thought he was a part of the loans department and started right in on why I needed a loan for kitchen equipment. It turns out, Noah gifted me the money without me realizing it and copped to it once everything was firmly purchased and installed. The finances came from the money he received from his father's estate. And since the money wasn't earned with integrity—he pilfered Everett's poor mother while during their short tenure together—he wanted to donate it to a good cause. Both he and Everett agreed the bakery was a good one.

Noah's cheek rises on one side as he sheds a crooked grin. "After our hand in Mora's arrest last month, the calls started pouring in. I've got a few investigations going."

"*Ohh.*" I lean in, intrigued by this sexy detective seated before me. "Anything juicy?"

"Yeah." Lainey leans in as well. "Who's having an affair with whom? Are you doing any stakeouts?" She jumps in her seat, practically foaming at the mouth wanting answers.

Noah holds out a hand, his chest thumping with a laugh. "I can't divulge the details of my cases. And, believe me, they are far from juicy. But I can say a few of them involve those garage burglaries." He points to Lainey. "Be sure to keep a good lock on that thing. Most of these thefts occurred by way of garage doors that are operated with an electronic remote."

She gasps, "That's all I've got. So not fair. It's as if the thieves of this world are always one step ahead." She looks at her phone in haste. "I'd better hustle. I've got to be at the library in a few minutes." She glances my way as she rises. "Any recommendations on what I should have for breakfast?"

"I put in a few chocolate croissants that—"

"Ah-ah!" She holds up her hand and stops me. "Say no more. Sold. In fact, I'll take two and have one for a snack later," she sings as she makes her way to the counter.

I give Noah's sleeve a quick tug. "Any leads on who killed Hunter?" Thankfully, I'm not a suspect in this one despite the fact I found his body. A thought occurs to me. "I'm not a suspect, am I?"

He winces as he warms my hand with his. "It's routine. But I promise, the captain doesn't think you had anything to do with it outside of the discovery of the body."

"Oh, cheese balls," I hiss as I snap my laptop shut. "Anyone else? Anyone who could have feasibly done this?"

"There's Bear."

"*Bear*?" I screech a little too loud, and a few women at the next table turn this way. They're tourists and most likely have no idea what carnage took place here last night. "That's terrible. Bear wouldn't hurt a fly. That's nothing but another dead end."

"Well"—Noah tugs at his collar—"he didn't shed a tear last night, but he did look upset. In fact, if I had to guess, he looked fighting mad."

That argument I witnessed between Bear and Hunter just a few minutes before I made the gruesome discovery comes to mind, and a breath locks in my throat at the thought of it.

"Lottie, what is it?" Noah leans in close, the tip of his head just an inch from mine, and his warm cologne permeates me with its warm scent.

"I—" A part of me can't do it. I know for a fact Bear would never kill Hunter. Why arm Noah with false evidence? "It was nothing. I'll do whatever I can to prove Bear's innocence. It's the least I can do after he moved heaven and earth to open this place in record time." Even if it means keeping his dark, *angry* secrets.

Noah squints into me as if prying into my thoughts. As if he could. But then, if I can see the dearly furry departed, and on occasion those once robed in flesh, maybe he can pry into my thoughts? I straighten in fear.

"I've got a juicy tip for you."

"Oh?" I'm right back to leaning in and swooning into those key lime green eyes, those kissable lips just inches from mine.

"I know of a couple of houses for rent side by side on Country Cottage Road."

"Ooh, that's a nice neighborhood. It butts right up to the woods. I just love that— *Hey*? Isn't that the street you live on?"

He nods, and that naughty grin is right where it's supposed to be.

"If you decide to take a look, call me and I'll join you. In fact, I can have my realtor set up an appointment if you like."

My mouth falls open at the thought of living in such close proximity to this alarmingly handsome man who has stolen my heart so quickly.

"I am more than interested. Let your realtor know we'll take a look as soon as we can." *We.* A content sigh expels from me. Deep down, I've always wanted to be a happy we. Although, we haven't actually spoken about the fact we're dating. Heck, I don't even know if you could call what we do dating. We're pretty good at kissing, though. My lips can't help but curve up at the sight of his.

"Good." He pats his hand over mine as he stands. "I'll follow up on some leads I've got concerning—" He tips his head toward the alley. It's probably wise not to shout Hunter's name after what happened. The last thing I want is for my bakery to be a landmark for murder, or a place too sad to visit. "Text me when you hear anything."

"Will do," I say as he takes off with a wave.

Oh shoot. I forgot to feed him and give him coffee. Everyone knows the way to a man's heart is through his stomach. Looks like I'm failing Boyfriend 101 right out the gate.

Speaking of boyfriends, I need to find a way to clear my ex's name.

Micheline and those teary eyes she had at the grand opening come to mind. Hey, wait a minute. She looked like she was grieving before poor Hunter ever bit the big one.

I head back to the kitchen to pull out my cookies and cheesecakes. I think in a couple of hours I'm going to make a deposit down at the bank. And while I'm there, I'll bring Noah a dozen fresh-baked chocolate chip cookies that I'm about to whip up just for him.

Look out, Noah Fox's stomach, I'm gunning for you.

I cringe at my own analogy considering the fact Hunter was shot to death.

Regardless, I hope Noah's heart is quick to follow his stomach.

I'm falling for him.

I just wish I knew exactly how he felt about me.

5

I was right.

The thick, sweet scent of the Cutie Pie Bakery and Cakery can joyfully be inhaled all the way down the street where I'm currently standing outside of Noah's office cradling a box of freshly baked chocolate chip cookies. But to my dismay, I'm not staring into the sea green eyes of that tall, dark-haired, and handsome private investigator. I'm staring into a cold hard sign that reads *closed* in glaring red letters.

And since Noah isn't here to partake in this warm batch of ooey gooey goodness, I decide to do the very next best thing with them. I don't waste any time trotting them into the bank.

The Honey Hollow Savings and Loans isn't too spacious inside, but it's always offered a warm, comforting feeling with its maroon carpet patterned with leaves, its brightly lit foyer filled with coffee urns, and a box of donuts open for any willing customer to enjoy. Just ahead of me, I see a hole in the wall and construction materials strewn about. I know for a fact Bear put this job off until the bakery was finished, and I feel a bit guilty over it.

I give a quick glance around. A handful of customers are being tended to at the teller windows, but I don't see Micheline.

A woman in a yellow pencil skirt and cashmere cardigan walks by with an arm full of files. "Can I help you?"

"Yes, actually. I was looking for Micheline Roycroft, but I don't see her. It wouldn't be her day off, would it?"

"Oh no, she's right next door in the loans department."

"Loans department. Right. Thank you," I say, scuttling my way back out. I know all about the loans department. That day I met Noah comes crashing back to me, and I can't help but smile just thinking about it. The day I met Everett comes barreling back, too, and I cringe at how up close and personal my entire head came with his nether regions. Both introductions were equally awkward, and yet they both led to what feel like genuine friendships. A part of me hopes that what Noah and I have blooms into so much more. After that New York debacle, I had sworn off men. Silly, I know. But here I am. Hoping to make it official with the cute boy down the street. And if I end up loving one of those rentals on Country Cottage Road, he will literally be the boy down the street two times over.

I head into the small, boxy room and spot Micheline and a couple of other people seated in makeshift cubicles. She's the only one without a customer at her desk, so I happily head on over.

"Hey, girl!" I say brightly and am suddenly mortified because the love of her life was just gunned down brutally less than twenty-four hours ago.

Micheline looks up with bloodshot eyes, her mouth pulled back in horror, and then just as quickly she softens as she stands and offers me a seat.

"What brings you here?"

"I come bearing gifts," I say with a grimace as I set the pink box in front of her. "Chocolate chip cookies." A lull of silences cuts through the air. "I know this is hard for you. It's hard for all of us. I'm really sorry. Hunter was my friend, too."

Her face pinches as if she might cry, and she snatches a few tissues out of the box in front of her and pushes them to her nose. "I know. I know it's hard for you, too." She offers a commiserating nod. "How is Bear?"

"He's with family. I texted him last night after I left, and he mentioned they'd be busy making arrangements today."

"I figured so." Fresh tears pour from her as she dabs them away with that growing wad in her hands. "I suppose it's for the best. Get that part over with." Her eyes congeal thick with tears. "How are you? How's the bakery?"

Micheline slouches over herself, her body looking far more fragile than I remember. If I didn't know better, I'd bet she was grieving far longer than a day.

"It's great. It's doing well. I mean, it's a few hours into the first day of business and the tourists and the townspeople really seem to enjoy it." I tug on a loose curl near my shoulder. "Can I ask if you had a chance to speak with Hunter last night, you know, before it happened?"

Micheline sighs as she looks to the ceiling. "I did end up finding him, but he was having a pretty heated debate with someone and I didn't want to interrupt. In hindsight, knowing how awful everything turned out, I wish I would have interrupted."

"I bet you had a lot to say." I tip my ear her way without meaning to. It's a natural tendency I have when I want to do my best to listen to someone. My mother says it's hardwired in me to do that.

"Oh, I did." She cocks her head as if none of it were good. "He had some troubles, and I wanted to help him as much as I could."

"Troubles?" I lean in. Micheline really is beautiful. I remember how close we grew while we dated the Fishers. I used to think she could have any guy she wanted, and I still stand by that statement. Of course, Hunter was a looker himself, as is Bear. But Bear's problem was that he knew it. And, if I'm being honest, Hunter knew it, too.

"Not dating troubles." She shakes her head as if ready to dispel any rumors from the start. "We were getting close, though." Her voice wobbles, and she adds another tissue to the collection in her hand. Her eyes hook to mine as she gives an exasperated sigh. "He had come to me asking for a loan. He didn't get it."

A loan? Micheline had to turn him down for a loan? That must have really put a pin in his ego.

"Is that why the two of you were having trouble? You looked pretty upset last night when I saw you. I didn't want to say anything, but you looked like you could have used a tissue then, too." My heart drums into my chest because I can't shake the feeling Micheline's walls are about to crumble, and all of the dark secrets she knows about Hunter are going to topple out.

"I could have. That's for sure." She cracks open the box and politely offers me a cookie first.

"No thanks. They're all for you." The rich scent of vanilla and chocolate permeates the air between us. It's too strong and far too delicious to ignore, so I don't blame her for diving on in.

"Mmm," she moans through a bite, her eyes rolling up toward her forehead. "I'm sorry, but this is bliss. I haven't eaten a thing all day. And, of course, I couldn't even think about dinner last night. You're a saving grace, Lottie. You always were."

"You're welcome." This is the part where I should probably wrap things up and leave, but I just feel so close to getting the answers that I need—answers that I didn't even know I wanted. "I hope you don't feel like I'm pushing, but is it true? Did the two of you have a disagreement? I mean, if you did, I want to be here for you. I can't imagine what that would feel like to leave things off with someone." It's true. I'm still her friend, and I would do anything to support her through this.

Micheline swallows hard and looks out the window to her left as an older surly man with silver hair loads drywall debris into his truck. I'm guessing he's one of the construction workers next door judging by the dirty white tee and matching pants. He has a tool belt on without anything attached. He turns slightly while wiping the sweat from his brow, and I note how ruddy his complexion is. I suppose hauling building materials in and out of the back all day would give anyone a great workout.

"Hunter and I had a lot of disagreements. But in the end, we were close to getting ourselves back on track." Her chest bucks, but she keeps her gaze firmly directed out of the window. "He didn't qualify for a loan from the bank, but I know he was asking Chuck for money, too." She nods toward the surly man outside.

"Chuck? Does he work for Bear, too?"

Bear has his own construction company, and Hunter was his second in command.

"No, that's the replacement Bear called in to finish up some of his overflow work. Chuck has his own construction company. Popov Construction." No sooner does she say it than he slams the door, and I see the oversized lettering across the door that reads *Popov Construction. We build it to last for life.*

"That's right. They were so busy with the bakery."

"Yes, exactly." She takes a deep breath, relaxing somewhat for the first time since I set foot in here.

"Did Chuck give Hunter the loan he needed?"

She shrugs as if she weren't certain of it. "Not that I know of. And if he were going to do it, well, it's too late for that now, isn't it?"

There's a note of anger in her tone, and it can't be denied. I've never seen Micheline so all over the place with her emotions. Not that the occasion doesn't call for it, but something is definitely off. First of all, she was upset before Hunter was brutally gunned down. I suppose a rocky relationship can do that to you, but still. So odd.

My brief wedding engagement comes to mind, and I quickly push it away. Curt and all of the grief he caused can stay in New York forever as far as I'm concerned.

"Hunter sounded pretty desperate," I whisper mostly to myself. "Hey, Micheline? What do you think made him so desperate for money?" I lean in, ear tipped her way in the event she feels an innate need to fill it with words—hopefully, the right ones.

Her features harden a moment as she looks right at me.

"I guess"—her mouth opens and closes as she quickly scoops up a stack of files over her desk—"I really need to get back to work." She hops out of her seat. "Thank you for the cookies, Lottie."

There's that. She takes off down the hall, and I hightail it out the door and into the icy autumn air just as Chuck Popov is about to climb into his truck.

"Excuse me, Chuck?"

He does a double take my way and lifts a bushy gray brow.

"You wouldn't have happened to have any dealings with Hunter Fisher, did you?"

A garble of unintelligible sounds emit from his mouth as he climbs into his truck shaking his head. The engine fires up in a moment as the truck expels a plume of smoke and drives off down the street.

And there he goes.

"Looks like I'm two for two."

"Two for two?" a female voice calls out behind me, and I turn to find freakishly tall, redheaded Collette Jenner standing before me on what appear to be stilts, i.e., expensive red-bottomed stilettos. She's donned one of those power pantsuits she's prone to wear in a deep shade of burnt orange. Collette works at some fancy PR firm in

Ashford, and I'm guessing she's through for the day. Lucky me.

She leans in with her nose twitching. "I bet you're two for two as in one man too many. I don't know who you think you are all of a sudden collecting boyfriends like they were playing cards, but stay away from mine." She sneers before speeding off in the opposite direction.

"And who would that be?" I call after her. I couldn't help it. Everett has told me countless times they are and will remain exes. Okay, so he may not have included the bit about remaining so, but he emphatically implied it.

"You know who he is, Lottie Lemon!" She turns around with fury in her eyes. "I'm warning you. Stay away."

I watch as she hops into her shiny black sports car and zooms off without so much as turning the ignition. Everything has always fallen into place for Collette—the looks, the cars, the careers, and the men.

Three out of four ain't bad.

She can't have Mr. Sexy. And not because he's mine.

It's because he doesn't want her.

I find myself standing in front of the window to Noah's office and touch my hand against the glass.

And I wonder if Noah wants me.

One thing is for certain—Micheline Roycroft knows exactly why Hunter was so desperate for money.

And I'm going to make sure I know exactly why, too.

6

The first few days at the bakery have been more than hectic. Usually when I finish up for the evening, I head straight home to Lainey's where I happily crash on the bed in the guest room and Pancake is happy to crash right along with me. He's made it no secret how much he's missed me these past few crazy weeks. But I plan on making it up to him soon with a trip to Just for Pets. For the last few months, each time I head over to stock up on his Fancy Beast pet food, I've brought him along. I always bring along his carrier, too, in the event a large dog decides it's hungry for *pancakes*. But so far, the need hasn't arisen, and Pancake seems to be more than content to peruse all the goodies. I'll admit to purchasing him a few new toys each time we're there. But I did manage to resist the cute cat costumes they have on display. When I presented the idea to him, along with an adorable little tutu, he shot me with death rays. I'm pretty sure he knew where that was going.

Noah and I have been hit-and-miss all week partially because I'm so busy with the bakery, but he too has been so very busy with all of his new cases, it makes me wonder if the best of what we were to have is already in the past. I would never want him to slow down because of me. I totally get not having time to do all the fun things. Hopefully, it's just a passing phase. A part of me was hoping he'd at least ask me on a date, but on this mundane Friday night, I've decided to take myself out.

Mom called an hour ago and asked if I would meet her at McMurry's Pumpkin Patch to pick out a few of the happy squashes and gourds for her bed and breakfast and, of course, I was more than happy to oblige. Nothing makes me happier than a cool fall night spent at Honey Hollow's famed questionably haunted pumpkin patch. The McMurrys play up the Halloween angle every year and wisely so. Their haunted hayrides are so famous you need to buy tickets weeks in advance before they sell out. They have a haunted maze, a haunted house, which is more of a series of trailers that have been welded together, and, of course, there are a ton of family activities for the younger set—games, petting zoo, bounce houses. It's a real party the entire month of October, and usually I'm here every single night soaking it all in.

The pumpkin patch is festooned with scarecrows in every shape and color all around the enormous farm, and they stand illuminated against the backdrop of a glowing purple night sky. There's a traditional pumpkin patch lot, and then there's the pick-it-yourself version, which leads you out into the acreage the McMurrys own. As far as the eyes can see, the cheery orange globes dot the landscape, and the surrounding trees have all shed their colorful leaves as stacks and stacks of hay are strewn about with people sitting on them, climbing on them, and taking an endless array of selfies. The air holds the slight scent of cinnamon, and I spot a cider booth not too far off from here. Nothing pairs better with a crisp, fall night than a steaming cup of cider. My feet are already headed in that direction when I stop dead in my tracks and gasp.

Standing next to the cider booth is a tall, lanky, hair-flipping two-timer that I'd know anywhere and yet loathe to see just about everywhere I spot him. It's Tanner Redwood handing some bleached blonde a cup full of apple cider goodness. His free hand is pressed into her lower back, and they're laughing it up as if they didn't have a plus one in the world—or more to the point, at how bamboozled he has my sister. As much as I want to boot scoot in that direction, and dump that scalding cider over his head, I don't feel like racking up assault charges for accidentally blistering the blonde next to him. Him I might consider doing a tiny stint in the slammer for. A misdemeanor in exchange for getting him out of Lainey's life for good seems like a reasonable exchange. But I think better of it and do the next best thing—take a few clandestine pictures.

A pair of hands gives my ribs a quick tickle from behind, and I scream as I bounce my way to safety.

I turn around to find my mother laughing her head off.

"You about gave me a heart attack. Don't ever do that again."

She's quick to wave me off. She's donned her favorite denims and is swaddled in a flannel printed down jacket. My mother is forever the fashionista and would never miss an opportunity to dress for pumpkin picking success. I've donned my favorite knee-length boots, denim, and flannel as well, and I can't help but think I got the memo from my mother, but a quick look around the vicinity proves everyone in Honey Hollow got the memo. A flannel and jeans are your typical uniform around these parts anyway.

"Well, I didn't know how else to break your spell. You looked like you were intensely doing something on your phone. Texting the good detective, perhaps? Or if the rumor mill is correct, was it the good judge?" That smile of hers is quickly replaced with a pinched frown, her fists digging into her hips with disapproval. "Lottie Lemon, how could you keep the fact you have two budding romances away from me? And I had to hear it from the grapevine no less!"

A horrific groan comes from me as we make our way toward the pumpkin patch. "I'm not even sure if I have one romance, Mother. Besides, who is busy spreading rumors about my love life? Please tell them I think they can use something constructive to do during waking hours. The bakery is hiring, by the way, so feel free to spread that rumor. It happens to be true."

"You know I will, honey," she says, grabbing one of the free wagons they offer to help haul your load.

When my sisters and I were little, we used to make our mother push us around in circles until we were dizzy and fell right off those red wagons. I've often wondered if that's where Meg got her love for tossing herself about so violently. She's at the top of her game, though. I've heard people place more bets on her matches than any other female wrestling pairing, so there's that.

Mom holds up a pleasantly plump, light peach Fairytale pumpkin for me to inspect.

"I love it," I say, taking it from her and setting it into the wagon. "Get at least three of those. There's something magical about them, and women especially just love them. You want to make sure your visitors feel good about every aspect of the B&B. In Business 101, I learned that depending on how you made your customers feel was ninety percent the deciding factor on whether or not they came back. Although, in my case, I'm sure the tasty treats have something to do with it. I hope."

She chortles at the thought. "I know so. That's all anyone's talking about is that grand opening of yours." She winces as she says it before picking up a few small pumpkins tiny enough to fit in the palm of your hands.

"Get at least thirty of those," I say, taking in a lungful of the earthy soil beneath us. "And you don't have to hide it. I know exactly why my grand opening was the talk of the town. Poor Bear hasn't even responded to my messages. He's really broken up about losing his cousin like that. And who wouldn't be?"

Mom shudders as the evening grows dark and sinister around us. "I just ran into Dee Fisher at the florist. She said poor Hunter didn't have anyone but them. I didn't realize his parents had passed away a few years back."

"Wow." I'm stunned to hear it. "I didn't realize that myself. I bet that's why he had no one to turn to for the loan," I say that last bit under my breath, mostly to myself.

"Loan?" Mom startles. "Come to think of it, he did speak to Wallace extensively about his finances."

"Hunter did?" I take a few steps toward my mother in haste. "What did he say? Was he looking for a loan? Why did he need the money?" Who knew it would be my mother of all people who had the potential to crack this case wide open?

Mom scoffs while leading us over to the gourds. "Wallace and I don't make it a practice to mix business and pleasure." She hikes her shoulder my way suggestively. "We much more prefer the pleasure."

"Mother! I'd cover my ears if my hands weren't filled with acorn squash at the moment."

"What? You should be happy for me that I've found someone so handsome and eager to please me. Just like I'm happy that you found two someones looking to occupy your time. You don't know how thrilled I am to know you won't really grow to be some old cat lady. You need a man in your life to spice things up." She rocks her chest my way, and I'm quick to avert my gaze. "Someone to heat the sheets with on those cold winter nights. Speaking of winter, I need to have a new heating system put in at the B&B."

A thought comes to me, and I can't catch my next breath I'm so excited. "We should double date!"

"What?" She blinks at the curveball I've just thrown at her. "A double date?" Her eyes expand to the size of baseballs. "Why, that's a fabulous idea! We could bring Lainey and Tanner in on the fun. I couldn't think of any better way for the Lemon women to kick off their brand new love lives than together."

"No, not Lainey." I glance to the area where I spotted Tanner with his optional plus one, but they're no longer haunting the vicinity. "I think she and Tanner are on the rocks. But don't tell her I told you so," I'm quick to warn. My mother would spoil the surprise before I ever got home as far as Tanner's inadvertent exit strategy to leave my sister goes. "Just the two of you and Noah and me."

I couldn't think of a better way to do a little inadvertent strategizing myself. I've been chomping at the bit for a date with Noah, and I don't see why I shouldn't ask him on one myself. I did ask him to that football game in

Ashford last month, and that totally counts even if we were secretly spying on Coach Hagan. But nonetheless, this will be another easy excuse to get together with him. Once he sees the potential value in gleaning all we can on Wallace, he'll happily go along—and hopefully be happy to spend time with me at the same time.

"In fact, I'll text him right now and see when he's free."

I step a few feet away while my mother busies herself filling that wagon to the brim. Just as my thumb is about to float over my screen, I spot an all too familiar scene at the cider booth, only this time it's not Tanner laughing it up with that bleached blonde of his—it's Noah and a leggy redhead who looks all too eager to snuggle up next to him. Her hand is on his arm, and her shoulder edges toward his chest as if she wanted far more of him than she's touching at the moment.

I've suddenly lost the urge to discuss Hunter's murder with Noah Fox.

Instead, I'm entertaining two new potential homicides.

7

A cold autumn night like this one usually requires a cup of cider or two to warm my bones, but the sight of Noah Fox two-timing me with some leggy redhead has my blood boiling enough to thaw the poles and cause apocalyptic devastation.

Mom chatters on behind me, and soon she's dragging that wagon we filled with pumpkins and gourds of every shape and size toward the cashier. I'm just about to join her when Noah looks my way and does a double take. He sidesteps away from the cackling hussy so fast you would think she were an official carrier of an airborne STD.

"Lottie!" he shouts with a wave, and I pretend not to see him as I scuttle my way to my mother. It's murky out.

The purple sky has darkened to a rich shade of navy, and the stars spray out overhead in their brilliant multitude.

Mom is busy chatting away with Ken McMurry, and I land shoulder to shoulder with her just as Ken offers to load our haul into the back of my mother's car.

"Lottie." Noah jogs up, out of breath. His cheeks look piqued as if he had exerted himself, but we both know it's because he's morbidly embarrassed because he was *caught*. "What are you doing here?" He sheds an easy grin, and it only makes me angrier.

How dare he be unaffected by the fact I saw him pawing over some redhead, even if she was the one doing the pawing. It matters not. He allowed it.

"I'm here with my mother. We were picking out pumpkins for the B&B. What are *you* doing here?" I tip my head his way, good and ready to listen in on whatever he has to say. I'm curious if this two-timer is also a liar. Most are.

"Thanks to Captain Turner, Detective Fairbanks invited me to help out with the investigation. You know, nothing official, but she thought it would be beneficial to exchange information."

My heart sinks because that's exactly what I was hoping to do with him. "And? Did you get anything useful?"

My bruised ego has quickly taken a back seat to my need to have my curiosity quenched. "Do you know why Hunter needed a loan?"

"Hunter needed a loan?" He leans in, and the heady scent of his cologne makes me feel dizzy. Just thinking about those kisses we've exchanged so freely has my head spinning and not in a good way. I feel like such a fool. I had no idea I was in some kind of an open relationship—some cheap fling that involved a lot of heavy kissing. Not that I minded the heavy kissing. That was sort of my favorite part.

"I don't know." I decide to play coy. "Did he?" I lift a brow his way. I am so not above playing these head games right along with him.

Mom bounces over breathless from the trek to her car. "Oh my goodness, we meet again, Detective Fox. Has Lottie mentioned the double date yet? Saturday night works for us. I just checked with Wallace." Her shoulders do that annoying shimmy thing again. Note to self: Buy this woman a lead coat for Christmas—and a *muzzle*. "Anyway, I have to run." She wrinkles her nose my way. "I just realized I'll need to ask one of my strong boarders to help carry all of these pumpkins out of my car. The last thing I need is my interior ruined. I've seen the way those things liquefy seemingly overnight." She presses a quick peck to my cheek. "Let me know what you decide. The two of you can pick the time and the place!" She wiggles her fingers at us as she's swallowed up by the night.

"Are we going on a double date?" Noah is back to sporting that crooked grin once again. There's an innate cockiness about him that's just too smug for me to handle at the moment, and I'm half-tempted to jump into my mother's trunk myself.

"I am. I don't know about you." I pluck my scarf out of my purse and wrap it around my neck. "So, were you enjoying clinking your cider with Detective Fairbanks?" I don't see why we should ignore the redheaded elephant at the pumpkin patch.

The scent of a floral perfume envelops us, and I turn to find Detective Ivy Fairbanks, stone-faced and staring me down.

"Carlotta Lemon." There's a smugness in her voice when she says my formal name. Funny, smugness seems to be catching these days. "I might be by your bakery sometime soon. I have a few questions we need to go over." She looks to Noah, equally as bored, and now I'm shocked he got her to laugh at all. "I'll see you in the morning, Fox. We'll start back here first thing." She takes off, and neither of us says anything. I might be a little smug myself at the thought that Noah didn't even bother saying goodnight to her, but then someone as confident, and let's not forget intimidating, as Ivy isn't insecure enough to let the absence of a goodbye mean a single thing. I wonder if Noah has been smooching with her, too, and as much as I don't want to go there, I can feel the word vomit ratcheting up my throat.

"Have the two of you kissed yet? You looked mighty friendly." Stupid, stupid me. I hate that I let my insecurities get the better of me. But I'm not surprised. It's practically my MO. No wonder all of my exes cheat on me. They can't get away from me fast enough to break things off properly.

Noah rumbles with a dark laugh as he swoops me into his arms and gently lands his lips to mine for a good ten seconds. Those soft, delicious lips sealed to mine feel like heaven. It feels like bliss with Noah, his mouth warming mine, his body solid against my own. Everything about him is pushing me over the edge. It takes all of my self-control not to dive my fingers into his thick hair.

He pulls back just enough for his *ivy* green eyes to glow my way, and I can't help but smile despite all of my lunacy.

"I save all of my kisses for you, Lottie Lemon."

My insides disintegrate, and every last cell in my body is swooning hard for the handsome fox with his arms wrapped securely around me right now.

His dark brows do a quick waggle. "Did I score an invite to that double date?"

"Maybe." I shrug. "I guess it depends if you're up for exchanging a little info on the case." It comes out hopeful. "I just have to clear Bear's name and get to the bottom of whoever killed Hunter. It feels like it's killing me as much as it's killed him."

Noah stiffens as he glances in the direction of the parking lot. "I can't, Lottie. I'm sorry. I promised Detective Fairbanks that I wouldn't share any details from the case. That was the deciding factor in allowing me to work with her. She doesn't want anything or anyone tainting the case. I get it. And"—he winces—"I know we already talked about this, but I want you safe. And if you're investigating this case, then I won't be able to stop worrying about you. There is a very real killer out there with a gun, and he or she is not afraid to use it."

I can't help but frown as I gently remove his arms from my person. "I get it." I shrug as I head over to the cider booth. I certainly don't need a man to make all of my cider dreams come true. Before I can toss a dollar into the basket, Noah beats me to it.

"It's on me." He sheds a pained smile. "Just like dinner will be Saturday night."

"Fine, but just know that I'm thoroughly annoyed that you're so unwilling to share details about something that's so important to me. How would you like it if a good friend of yours was gunned down right in the back of your own bakery on the night of its grand opening no less? You wouldn't." I don't hesitate answering for him. "You would resent the fact that I chose to keep Everett as my confidant instead of trusting your abilities to keep things quiet."

"Everett?" He balks with a laugh. "I don't think my former stepbrother would be too interested investigating a homicide." He pulls me in again gently with his arms. "You're not involving Everett, are you?" He's right back to wincing as if the idea pained him. I happen to know firsthand that Everett is an easy way to push his buttons. In that sense, it wasn't fair of me to go there.

"Not yet." I shudder just thinking about the fact he threatened to interrogate me over a dead squirrel no less!

"How about it? You, me, your mother, and her date, Saturday night?"

A tiny giggle works its way up my throat. "Fine. Just know that I'm the reason you'll be seated across from Wallace Chad that night. My mother mentioned that he and Hunter spoke about finances."

"You mentioned he was looking for a loan." He sighs, and a white plume blooms from his lips. "So, you know he was having trouble with money?"

"I'll tell you what I know if you tell me why you need to meet Detective Fairbanks here tomorrow morning. You do realize that a person can get lost for weeks in that haunted corn maze if they're not properly caffeinated before noon."

He barks out a laugh, and his teeth glisten like a string of glowing moons. "Yes, I do realize that. I guess there's no harm in telling you he was looking for employment here. Just helping out at night. Ken was busy, but we'll speak with him more in the morning about it."

"Oh. No, I didn't know that." I glance over to Ken and Molly who are helping organize a hayride. Not the terrifying one that they sell tickets for, but the run-of-the-mill kind you can take your toddler on and not fear nightmares for the next six years. "I guess he really was having trouble with money. I'll talk to Bear and try to find out how much he was paying him. I can't believe it wasn't enough."

"No, no, no." He tips his head back and moans mournfully before holding my gaze once again. "If you talk to Bear, and we talk to Bear about the same topic, it might spook him. Let me handle the investigation, and you worry about how many brownies to bake for the next day. Sound fair?"

I open my mouth to protest, then quickly close it. Working with the Ashford Homicide Division could be a big break for Noah. I'd feel terrible ruining it for him.

"Fair," I say it short and sweet, all the while crossing my fingers behind his back. No use in worrying him over something so silly. Bear is used to me asking all sorts of prying questions. And honestly, I might be the only person he feels comfortable opening up to. "So, Saturday night—Italian or Mexican? Or, of course, there's always the Honey Pot."

"I'm not above trying something new. Italian sounds a bit more neutral as far as the heat level goes."

"Sounds perfect." I lose myself in those evergreen eyes. "I've missed you."

A warm growl comes from him. "I've missed you, too. But I've been talking about you all week. Have your ears been burning?"

"No." I'm pleasantly surprised. "With Detective Fairbanks?"

"With Imogene Cross. She's the realtor who helped me find my own rental. She said she can let you into both houses on Sunday. And that happens to be my day off."

"Tell me the time and I'll arrange to be there." I'm giddy over the thought of moving to such close proximity to him. "So, this whole keeping secrets from each other thing isn't really going to last forever, is it?" My stomach cinches as soon as I get the words out. Regret thy name is Lottie Lemon.

"I'm not keeping secrets from you, I promise." He dots a sweet kiss over my lips, and I can't help but dig my fingers into the back of his thick dark hair. "No offense to you, Lottie. It's just business. As soon as anything can be made public, you will be the first to know."

A conciliatory sigh escapes me. "In that case, I wish both you and Detective Fairbanks luck in catching the killer quickly."

"Thank you." His finger swipes gently over my lips. "So, a double date, huh? Does that mean we're dating?"

My smile expands into the night. "I guess it does."

"I like that."

"I like that, too."

Noah bows in for another kiss, and we share something deeper, with far more meaning than a simple kiss could ever convey. My mouth opens for him, and what comes next spells out he's all mine more than words could ever hope. Too bad Ivy has pressured him into not sharing any details of the case with me, and sadly my aforementioned insecurities suggest I take this seriously. If Noah's not up for sharing details about the case, then neither am I. There's no way I want to help Ivy get a leg up on something only to have it backfire in my face. I'm sure she wouldn't hesitate to humiliate me in the process. I'm pretty sure I read that body language of hers loud and clear. She's interested in Noah Fox for more than just a few leads.

And that's exactly why I'll be investigating the rest of this case on my own.

No offense to Noah.

It's just business.

8

The next day, the bakery is still bustling well into the late afternoon. I blame those warm cinnamon rolls I just pulled out of the oven. I swear, each time I do that, all of Main Street empties out and floods into the Cutie Pie. Not that I mind. Actually, I cannot believe how much money we've made in less than a week. But as Lainey gently reminded me, the bakery is still in its honeymoon phase, and this is my chance to prove to my customers time and time again that our goods are as delicious as they smell. I need repeat business. I need for it to be this swamped and bustling a year from now. The last thing I want is to disappoint anyone. That, in fact, has always been my downfall.

It's almost five. The bakery is only open for one more hour and still no sign of catty Ivy wielding her badge in my face. Worse yet, she'll probably come in wielding my boyfriend at me. *Boyfriend.* There's that word again. We haven't fully discussed being exclusive, but he did say quite emphatically that he's saving all of those heated kisses for me. And, my God up in heaven, what sexy, smoldering, die-on-the-spot kisses they are. My insides do a cartwheel just thinking about them.

The bell to the bakery jingles, and my heart stops cold once I spot that all too familiar face. It's not Ivy or Noah. It's—Hunter?

"Hey, Lot." His voice strums my way as his features sag, and I come to.

"Bear." I rush over and wrap my arms tight around him before motioning to the staff that I'll be taking a break. "For a second I thought you were Hunter." I shake my head up at him, my eyes flooding with tears. "I'm so sorry about everything you've been through. I can't imagine the pain you're in right now."

His cheek flinches. "Thanks. I appreciate it." He looks around, and a sigh expels from his enormous chest. "This was the last place I saw him alive. It feels like five minutes ago. If I try hard enough, I can imagine that he'll walk right through that door grinning at me."

My heart breaks just hearing it.

The bell chimes again, and we turn to find Everett striding in, clad in a midnight-colored suit, his dark hair slicked back, and he twitches the slightest smile when he sees me.

Just as I'm about to greet him, a stunning brunette strides in behind him, thin as a rail, and stilettoes that practically make her touch the ceiling. Her chestnut-colored hair is taut in a bun, and she's wearing gold-rimmed glasses. A briefcase sits tucked under her arm. She wastes no time in striding over along with Everett.

Bear leans in. "Hope you don't mind, but I decided to meet with my new attorney here."

I suck in a quick breath as I look to Everett's female companion, and now that I think about it, I recognize her from that day the Simonson sisters took me to court.

"Fiona Dagmeyer." She's quick to shake Bear's hand. "Why don't we take a seat."

"Oh, sure," I say, pointing to an empty table by the window. "I can bring you coffee and some apple berry cobbler I just pulled out of the oven." I tip my head toward Bear. "I'll bring a few brownies to get you through it as well."

"No thanks." Bear picks up my hand carefully. "Just sit by my side. That's all the help I need to get me through this."

"I'll do whatever you ask."

"No, you won't," Fiona corrects with a curt smile that says something nasty far more than it ever does something nice. "I prefer to speak with my clients alone. I find when they're around family or friends they seem to want to embellish to save themselves of embarrassing truths. I don't have time for any of that."

"That's fine." I shake my head at Bear. "The two of you take a seat there, and Everett and I will sit at another table. I'll still be here for you."

Bear and Fiona head to the table near the window, and I'm slow to take a seat with the handsome judge in front of me.

"I'll get you some coffee," I say, batting my lashes up at him nervously. "In fact, I'd better check on those pies I have in the oven. There's so much to do before I close up for the night. I'm sure you understand."

I try to take off, and he quickly steps in front of me, blocking my path.

"Lemon." He points to the empty table near the door. "It's time."

I frown up at him. "I don't want it to be time. Can't you see I have nothing to hide? This little interrogation of yours is completely uncalled for."

"Lottie." His brows knot up. "You're incriminating yourself with your uncharacteristic behavior. You do realize I'm not going to hurt you. And I'm not turning you over to the police."

"It's not the police I'm worried about." It's men with nets that scare me. Ever since I was old enough to realize my gift was far from normal, I was petrified I'd end up in a mental institution somewhere. Just me in a straitjacket and a thousand critters from yesteryear. It's enough to make me go mad just thinking about it.

Everett lands a warm hand over my back and ushers us to the table as we take our seats.

He leans in, and the warm scent of his cologne tickles my senses. It's a bit spicier than the one that Noah wears but equally intoxicating. There's just something about cologne that does it for me. It might as well be a love potion—I respond that aggressively to it. A part of the reason is that my father wore his Old Spice liberally. Mom gifted my sisters and me each a bottle a few years back for Christmas, and we called it Dad in a Bottle. I guess that's why I love musky scents on men. Suddenly, everything just feels right with the world.

Everett takes a breath as if he too were girding himself. "What are you really afraid of?"

"You judging me." That, and psychotropic medications being force-fed down my pie hole. I would be the worst patient ever. They really would need to tie me to a bed.

A warm laugh bounces from him—a rarity in and of itself. "That's what I do by trade. I judge." His features harden. "But I won't judge you as a person. Now, walk me through it. You thought you saw a squirrel coming in through the front door."

"It was getting pretty warm in here with all of those bodies." Speaking of which, my body heat index spikes twenty degrees, and I can feel a bite of sweat erupting under each arm. "I hadn't eaten all day. Can you believe it? All of those fudgy brownies right in my face and not one bite." Truth. "Anyway. I guess it wasn't a squirrel after all. I'm just too embarrassed to tell you what it really was." A flare of heat rips through me as I spew an entire catalog of lies.

"What was it?"

Everett looks every bit the concerned friend. It's amazing to me that just a month ago I was swatting his behind with my forehead, and boy did I ever annoy the living heck out of him with those fancy face maneuvers. And yet here we are, chatting in my brand new bakery—about the curse that's finally about to take down my life.

I clear my throat. "It was a dust ball." It comes out lower than a whisper.

"A what?" He shakes his head in disbelief.

"You know, a little mini dirt devil. A tiny tornado of unhygienic fun. My mother always called them squirrels. They just come in and whip right through the house, embarrassing the socks off my mother and me." My face heats to unsafe levels. I'm positive you could light a cigarette right off of the tip of my nose. In fact, if Noah were here, I'd give him one big red-hot kiss just to get away from his snooping ex-stepbrother.

Everett sinks back in his seat. That look on his face is locked somewhere between anger and disappointment, a sure sign he's not buying the dirty load I'm trying to sell him.

"A dirt devil." He nods. "And you expect me to believe that a whirlwind of dust and debris—less than a foot tall—had the power to maneuver its way through a forest of bodies and make its way out the back—in a bakery with virtually no breeze." He cocks his head to the side as if volleying the dirty ball back in my court.

"Yes?"

"Lemon." He closes his eyes a moment, and for a second I contemplate running out the door. I can always cite female troubles. Men never like to hear the word *menstruation*. Actually, it not only might scare Everett off, it might clear out the bakery in record time. Of course, that would be another lie. And now that I'm dancing on a ball of flat-out lies, I'll have to keep adding to them just to keep myself from falling. Soon I'll be an astronaut who needs to check on the space station. A secret assistant to the President. My den of deceit knows no bounds.

"Let's try this another way." Everett sounds exactly as stern and in command as he did that day in court. "What do you think the repercussions would be if you told me the truth?" He gives a slight shake of the head. "Please don't bother elaborating on the dirt devil. I've already determined that was simply a cover in hopes I'll leave right this minute and buy you a broom."

A tiny laugh bubbles from me. There's just something about Everett that puts me at ease. "Fine." I swallow hard, knowing full well it's not fine. "But first, I have to tell you that what you're about to hear, only one other person on the entire planet is apprised of." I'm hoping that alone will give him pause.

"Go on." His finger calls to me as if beckoning me to get to it already.

"Not even my best friend, *Keelie*," I whisper in hopes he can see the severity.

"That's fine. I won't tell her. I promise I won't tell a soul without your permission." His gaze remains secure over mine.

Bear and Fiona head over, and I'm flooded with relief. Every last molecule in my body has just exhaled. I bolt up, and Everett is slow to follow.

"Well?" I ask the two of them. "What's the verdict?"

Fiona rides her gaze over me from head to toe, and judging by that nonplused look on her face, I gather she's not too impressed.

"Mr. Fisher"—she nods to Bear—"I'll be speaking with you soon. Think about the things I said and implement them."

Bear scratches at the back of his neck. "Will do."

She looks to Everett, and something akin to a genuine grin blooms on her face. "Essex, I'll be up late." She gives a sly wink before heading out the door.

"Up late?" I gawk as I give him a slight shove on the arm. "Don't tell me you're still dipping a toe into Dagmeyer infested waters."

"Not a toe." A dirty grin blooms on his face. "And not any other body part either. We're exes, Lemon. When I say something, you can count on the fact I'm telling the truth."

I suck in a quick breath and swat him over the arm once again.

Bear offers me a spontaneous hug. "I've got to run. It's been a long day."

"Yeah, sure." I bite down hard over my lower lip because there are still so many questions I want to ask him. "Hey, Bear? What kind of things did Fiona ask you to implement?" I'll start easy. Warm him up a bit.

"I need to buy a suit in the event this escalates any further. I'm innocent, but she said people are hungry for answers. I guess she's heard enough rumors that Hunter and I weren't exactly on friendly terms the last few weeks."

"Did he ask you for a loan?" I regret the words as soon as they sail from my mouth. So much for warming him up.

Bear ticks his head back as if it were ridiculous, but there's something in his eyes that says it's not. "Yeah, he asked. But I'm tapped so he didn't get it." He pinches his eyes shut a moment.

"Do you know if he asked Chuck Popov for a loan?" Micheline already suggested as much, but I figure square one is the best place to start as far as this conversation goes.

Bear winces. "How do you know this?" he whispers before rolling his eyes to the ceiling. "Yeah, he asked. The kid asked everybody. Nobody gave him anything, Lot. Especially not Chuck." He glances over my shoulder a moment at Everett before leaning in. "I asked Chuck not to give him anything, and in exchange I told him I'd make sure he got the bids when I backed out."

"At the bank?"

He nods. "And other jobs. I didn't want anyone feeding Hunter's need for green speed."

"Why?" I'm suddenly ravenous to know the answer.

He shakes his head. "Because nobody needs that much money, Lot." Everett clears his throat, and Bear's chest expands with his next breath. "I'll talk to you some other time, Lot. Funeral's on Sunday. I'll text you the details."

"Please do," I say as he speeds out the door.

Everett takes an enormous breath, and I swear I can see the judgment ready to pour out of him. "How did you know that kid needed a loan?"

"Never you mind." I look past him for signs of Ivy whom I've quickly adopted as my nemesis. Technically, that would be Naomi, Keelie's twin, but since Naomi isn't trying to staple Noah to her side, she's been evicted from the coveted position.

"Lemon, are you investigating Hunter's murder? Both Noah and I don't think—"

I hold a hand up between us. "I don't care what you think. Hunter was my friend, and Bear still is—sort of. Anyway, I'm being cautious so no need to worry."

He rocks back on his heels. "If you don't care about what I think, then you shouldn't have a problem letting me know what had you running out the back door that night. You found a body, Lemon. And to be honest, I think maybe you're too close to the situation or you'd see that there might be some importance in your own timeline of events leading up to the gruesome discovery."

"Ugh. You are relentless, you know that? And you're just as obnoxious as you were that day I met you in the coffee shop. If I recall correctly, you wouldn't tell me your name. Your *name*. And you're asking me to divulge something extremely private and quite painful to admit."

"What are you talking about?" His voice hikes an octave to match mine. "You said you saw a squirrel bolting through the place and followed it to a dead man."

"And you didn't see it!" I smash a finger into his granite-hewn chest. So not fair. Everett has the face and the body of a god. Lucky for me, so does Noah.

"You didn't see it either," he barks, and my adrenaline hits its zenith.

"Yes, I *did*," I spit the words in his face. "I saw a dead squirrel that once belonged to Hunter Fisher himself. A dead *pet*. It's what I always see before something very, very sinister happens to its previous owner. Are you happy?" I snip as I whip off my apron and speed through the kitchen. I tell the staff I'll be back to close up as I snatch my keys off the rack and race to my car that just so happens to be parked right over the spot Hunter breathed his last breath.

"Lemon, wait," Everett riots as he barrels out after me. But it's too late. I'm already racing off into the night.

I've never seen Everett so full of emotion—his heated anger matching mine. And then I remember him mentioning that he had his ways of getting information out of just about anyone. It was his gift.

I shake my head as a dull laugh pumps from me.

Everett wasn't angry with me. He was manipulating me to get what he needed.

Well played, Everett. Well played.

I pull out of the alley and spot Ivy Fairbanks heading into the bakery with a dutiful Noah by her side.

But I don't stop. I drive all the way to my sister's. There's only so much torment I can take for one night.

Everett promised he wouldn't tell a soul.

I kept my end of the bargain. Let's see if he keeps his.

9

In keeping with this seemingly new tradition of having my sanity disband at some point in the latter half of the day, my mother and her questionable suitor are seated across from Noah and me at Mangia, Honey Hollow's premier Italian restaurant which has write-ups in three national newspapers.

Noah picked me up from Lainey's, looking exceptionally comely tonight with a dark inky suit and a slick black tie to match. His hair is thick and glossy as if it were still damp from the shower, and the musky scent of his cologne made me want to grab him by the tie and trail off into the woods with him. Under no sane circumstances should we be waiting for our meals to arrive while discussing politics of all things with my mother's formidable boy toy. Sure, he's handsome for a silver fox, but there's a hint of something wily in his eyes that I can't quite pinpoint. His movements are too fluid, and his face is peppered with white hairs that look decidedly like a briar patch. Side note: Both Everett and Noah have a comfortable amount of dark stubble on their blessed by God faces, but it looks soft and inviting. Wallace here looks like a prickly cactus. I don't see how my mother could stand to make out with him.

Oh my *God*.

I bolt upright as if I had just been shot. She's not making out with him, is she?

Mom gives me a slight kick from under the table. "So Lottie, why don't you tell us all how it feels to finally run the bakery of your dreams? You've been waiting for this moment all your life." She offers a crimson-lipped smiled to both Noah and Wallace. "My daughter has been obsessed with baking ever since she got her hands on an Easy Bake Oven when she was three. Of course, all the girls used it." She grimaces at the memory. "Meg would toss a little mud in for flavor. But not my Lottie. She only uses the finest ingredients."

She winks my way, and I can feel my face heating. I've never done well with compliments in general. Truth be told, there's nothing more that makes me want to duck under this table and bury my face in my purse. It's been a long-standing problem of mine. My therapist, back in New York, suggested it was a byproduct of the fact I far more prefer rejection. She claimed that I don't actually believe the generous statements offered my way, that, in fact, I infer it to be mocking and satirical. My God, she is so right on the money. But this is my mother, and I know for a fact she would upsell me to a tree if she had to. So I take my therapist's sage advice on how to handle any kind words slung my way and say a simple thank you.

"Speaking of the bakery"—I start in on a perfect segue to Hunter and his financial woes—"I still haven't quite gotten over the trauma of having a homicide occur on day one."

The waitress comes with our dishes, and I grunt at the fact she's just ruined my momentum. Wallace isn't even looking at me right now. He's practically salivating over the chicken Parmesan they've set in front of him. I can't help but twitch my nose at the sight. My father once said never trust a man who orders chicken when there is steak on the menu. Noah moans approvingly as his steak Toscano is set before him, and I brush my shoulder to his, proud to have him by my side. Both my mother and I opted for the lighter fare, angel hair with Alfredo and shrimp.

Noah looks tenderly at me, and if I didn't know better, I'd swear we were having a moment. "I'm sorry you had such a dark event the night of the grand opening." His dimples press in, and I'm openly swooning at the king by my side. Why are my mother and her prickly pear here again? Oh, right.

"Yes." I take a deep breath, looking to Wallace. "It was quite a trauma. Did you know him very well?" I ask at the precise moment he indulges in a mouthful of chicken. He didn't even wait for my mother to place her napkin on her lap. I'm guessing his table etiquette is indicative of every other aspect of his life. He will always come first. And anyone who won't put my mother first is last in my book. She might as well give him his walking papers tonight, because judging by the way he's plowing through his meal—

Noah leans over, his mouth set directly over my ear, and my insides melt like butter on a griddle. "You're glaring."

I look up at him wild-eyed before bouncing in my seat and composing myself once again. "Your food looks wonderful, Wallace." Take two. "I came this close to ordering the chicken myself." Lies, all lies.

"Mmm." He lifts his fork as he swallows down a mouthful.

"Did you know Hunter Fisher?" I look right into his eyes, and my mother gasps, waving her hand at me as if she were gunning to swat me.

"Lottie Kenzie Lemon. You do not speak of the deceased while others are trying to enjoy their meal. It's bad enough you brought it up at dinner." She shudders, her narrowed beams of disapproval still set my way. "Noah, I promise you that I brought her up better than that. Lottie is always so rife with sparkling conversation. I don't know what's happened to her tonight."

Noah's chest bounces with a quiet laugh. "It's quite all right. I've already been treated to Lottie's sparkling conversation. And I rather enjoy her natural curiosity." He tilts his head while giving me the side eye, and I'm betting he's onto me. Crap. This was going to be my great find. My very own sparkly new suspect.

Noah reverts his gaze to Wallace. "So answer the question," he spits it out with a friendly grin. "Did you know Hunter Fisher?"

Wallace gives an eager nod while washing down his food.

Figures. I pry and nothing happens. Noah asserts his male prowess, and suddenly Wallace is so eager to speak he's practically choking on his food.

"I tried to work with the kid." His eyes flit to the depths of the room, and something about that ocular move raises my suspicions. He's thinking about something, and I want to know what. "The kid didn't have two dimes to rub together. It's a little tough to put a portfolio together when you're broke." He barks out a laugh while toasting us with his wine, and my mouth falls open, incredulous.

Anger is usually not my friend, but in this instance, it might be all I need.

"*Hey*"—I play up the affronted angle—"Hunter was a great person. Sure, he wasn't as financially savvy as yourself—" A good ego stroke always works with narcissistic men like Wallace. "But you could have helped him out, you know. Maybe got him started by giving him a loan?"

"*Lottie!*" Mom's fire engine red lips round out in a perfect O.

"It's fine." Wallace lifts a finger. "I actually looked into a loan for the kid." There's a bleak look in his eyes as if it didn't go so well. "Sometimes these things don't pan out."

Ha! Knew it. There is a connection between Wallace and Hunter's incessant need for green.

"So, how does that work? I mean, the loan process. If I needed a loan for the bakery, would I just go to you?"

Noah cuts me a quick look and gives a slight nod as if to say good work, and I can't say I'm not gloating a bit at the moment.

Wallace blows out a breath as if considering this. "It's not an easy process, but since I know you"—he leans in toward Mom—"and I *know* your mother..." Eww. "I can see about pulling a few strings."

Mom coos and chortles as if those strings were directly connected to her body. Double *eww*.

Noah clears his throat. "What's the name of the financial institution?" There's a hardness in his voice that has Wallace stiffening, so I give his knee a knock with mine, hoping he'll take a hint. "I mean, I'm looking for office space, and I can certainly use a leg up."

"Martinelle Finance," Wallace is quick to answer. "I've used them for several projects." His demeanor darkens.

We finish up with our meals, and soon Wallace and my mother are off to the late showing of some action adventure film at the Cineplex. I'm guessing that was not my mother's pick. He is so into pleasing himself it sickens me to think what goes on behind closed doors.

Noah and I take an inadvertent casual stroll down Main Street and end up at the huge fountain in the middle of Founders Square. He's held my hand every step of the way, and it's all I can do not to pull him into some dark alcove and have my way with him. To say Noah gets my heart pitter-pattering wouldn't be skimming the surface of what this man does to me. Parts of my body are quivering that haven't quivered in a good long while, and if I pant any faster, he's going to think I need a medic.

Noah pulls me in, and my fingers glide down his tie as the moonlight washes him silver. The air is icy, and the wind blows the oak leaves around us like glittering confetti.

"Lottie Lemon." He doesn't smile when he says my name. In fact, there's a note of suspicion buried there somewhere. "You're investigating Wallace, aren't you?"

"Aren't *you*?" I tease. "I mean, professionals like Detective Fairbanks and yourself certainly must already have a bead on Wallace Chad by now." I can't help but flutter my lashes up at him. I might as well soften the blow to his ego with a little flirtation, and I do plan to spend the rest of the evening indulging in every flirtation possible with this shining moon god. The fountain rushes behind us, and the scent of night jasmine still clings to the air despite the fact autumn is well underway.

His affect darkens as his expression turns serious on a dime. "We do," he deadpans. "We also know that Martinelle Finance has a reputation, and they may be dealing in dicey waters. We found that out two days ago." He brushes a stray hair from my cheek tenderly with his thumb. "I know this is going to be hard for you to hear, and just because you hear it doesn't mean you'll listen—but we don't need you in this investigation, Lottie. You're right. We are professionals," he says it sweetly enough, but it puts a pin in an ego I didn't even know I had. "You keep baking pies, and brownies, and every cookie under the sun. You're good at it. That's what you do. This homicide investigation is what I do. And I'm good at it. So please, trust me to catch the bad guys and don't go looking for them yourself. And I know you don't care to hear that, but I couldn't live with myself if anything happened to you."

Every last ounce of me sighs with defeat. A part of me wants to push aside the investigation for the night, push aside our differences in how that investigation should be run, and by who, and just take in the splendor of this god before me. I want to do a million carnal things with this beautiful man, but I can't run away from this. Hunter meant something to me, and just because I've been bested doesn't mean I'm going to let it go.

"Okay, you are a professional, and my time and talents are better served mixing up cake batter and putting your favorite chocolate chip cookies in the oven." I give a cheeky smile, and it's genuine. "And thank you for sharing that tidbit with me. I know it's not easy for you to share information, especially now that Detective Fairbanks has taken a blood oath from you." I glower at the mention of her name.

"Good." His hand presses into my lower back, closing the distance between us. "If we weren't having such a big day tomorrow, I'd invite you to my place right now." There's a glint of something decidedly naughty in his eyes, and I'm suddenly ready to eschew anything on my calendar tomorrow to explore the night in the *Fox's den.*

Then it hits me, and I tip my head back and groan.

"I forgot all about the funeral in the morning."

"And I hope you didn't forget about my real estate agent."

I suck in a quick breath, hopping up on the balls of my feet with excitement. "The rentals! I did forget all about them. But now that you've reminded me, I'm thrilled about it." I cringe a moment. "It feels so wrong to be excited about anything tomorrow."

"I know." He brushes a quick kiss to my lips, and my heart slaps hard against my chest as if it were trying to get out and get a kiss for itself. Noah Fox has pillow-soft lips, and I could eat them for breakfast, lunch, and dinner.

I'm not sure why, but there is a very real soul-crushing need for me to ask him about us, who we are, what we mean to one another. It sounds so silly, so schoolgirl to ask something as ridiculous as *are you my new boyfriend?* But inquiring minds would like to know if he's interested in something more than just a few kisses.

"What are you thinking?" he whispers into my ear, his lips softly outlining my temple, and the sensation alone has me outright moaning.

"I'm thinking if you keep doing that I'll need to take a dip in the fountain to cool off." I pull back and look into his heated gaze. Noah is feeling something primal for me, and every last part of me is right there with him. "And I was wondering if"—my mouth remains open, but the words get lodged in my throat—"um, maybe we could grab lunch tomorrow. I really do enjoy spending time with you."

"That sounds like a perfect plan."

Lunch? That's the best I could do? I frown over at him without meaning to. At least I'll get to eat one of my favorite meals, and if Noah takes me to his place, I might get to take a bite out of something else my mouth is watering for.

Noah cups my cheeks and pulls me in gently while landing those magic lips over mine. There is a sweetness to Noah's kisses, a willingness to linger, and we do. Noah and I kiss in front of that fountain as if we were offering up a nonverbal proclamation to the townspeople of Honey Hollow. We are saying here we are, together, and that's how we'll remain. We are real. We are falling hard for one another. The only thing I can't say with certainty is whether or not we're officially together. I've never felt this way about anyone before, and seeing that I've been engaged before, that's saying a lot.

Noah has blown the doors off any expectations I might have had for the opposite gender. He's blown the doors off what I thought I knew about the boundaries of my feelings, and that closed door to my heart has been taken right off the hinges.

Yes, I will give Noah his space as far as the investigation is concerned, but only so he doesn't bump into mine.

Noah mentioned that Martinelle Finances may be dealing in dicey waters. And if he's not looking to assist me in delving in further, I know a certain judge who owes me a favor for wrangling out the deepest, darkest secret from me.

Noah is right. He can ask me a lot of things, but it doesn't mean I'll listen.

And when it comes to solving Hunter's murder, I sure as heck won't.

10

Honey Hollow Covenant Church is packed to maximum capacity as the entire town shows up to bid farewell to one of its own. The funeral is brief, and both Bear and his mother offer up moving eulogies. But once they roll that video montage of Hunter's beautiful life, there isn't a dry eye in the house. Then just like that, the service is over.

Keelie threads her arm through mine as the bodies disappear and the sanctuary begins to drain. "That was beautiful, Lottie. If by chance I happen to die before you, please make sure to vet any photos my mother is willing to toss into the pictorial. That picture with Hunter's bedhead made me cringe. Rest assured, if anything untimely should happen to me and things at my funeral do not go as instructed, I'm not above ditching paradise to commence a good old-fashioned haunting."

"Duly noted, and, might I add, more than a little morbid considering the venue."

Keelie openly scowls at someone seated near the back, and I crane my neck to get a better look. "Can you believe he brought her?"

"Who brought whom?" No sooner do I say it than I spot them, and my heart lurches in my chest.

Noah offers a quick wave, along with what looks to be an apologetic smile, as a very unimpressed Detective Fairbanks stands dutifully by his side.

"That's funny. He didn't mention anything about her last night."

A light tap lands on my shoulder, and I turn to find the good judge nodding solemnly my way. Keelie spots her sister and takes off singing hello in such an alarmingly cheery tone half the congregation turns to inspect her. But that's Keelie. Nell always says you can't keep a good Keelie down. And she's definitely right about that. Knowing Keelie, she'd come back to haunt us just to say hello.

"Everett! What a surprise." And as quick as the joy of seeing him comes, it dissipates once I realize what he knows. My cheeks heat on cue.

"Lemon." He bows slightly. "My condolences."

"Accepted." I frown up at him because a part of me is waiting for him to whisk me away to some psychiatric facility for a prompt and necessary evaluation.

"Collette asked me to join her. She was extremely distraught so, of course, I couldn't say no."

"I bet she was." That woman never had a kind thing to say about Hunter. She's simply using his funeral to get into Mr. Sexy's pants. "So? How are you doing with the news I shared?"

He pulls back with confusion, and regret takes over his features. "Honestly, I don't know what to make of it. And, that's why I was hoping to talk to you this afternoon. I think I need you to elaborate."

"So you can firm up the case against me to have me committed? No thank you." I glance back to where Noah and his date were just a few minutes ago, but they've done a disappearing act. Probably outside inspecting the casket for clues before they bury poor Hunter. "But since you pulled something so intimate from me—a feat no other human has ever achieved before—" I told Nell myself, and that was willingly. Everett offers the hint of a smug grin. "I'd like to ask a favor of you. I need you to meet me in Ashford sometime this week."

"Stepping out for a clandestine meeting behind my stepbrother's back so soon? I'm intrigued. Where are we meeting? Just a heads-up. I prefer hotels to motels."

"Ha-ha. You're not funny. I'll text you with the details. Do me a favor, though, and try not to look so official. You're downright intimidating in a suit." He breaks out into an outright grin. "We'll have to pretend to be a couple going in for a loan. And it has to be believable."

"A couple looking for a loan?" Gone is any trace of a smile, and he's right back to being his intimidating self. "It sounds like you're investigating. What's in this for me?" He folds his arms across his chest as if we were suddenly in the boardroom going over hostile negotiations.

"This is a prepaid venture. I handed you the secrets of my soul on a silver platter, remember?"

He leans in, stern. "I want more. A full and thorough examination from A to Z. I need to know when this began, how often it occurs, and if you're hearing voices."

"Oh? Is that what the psychiatrist you contacted suggested you look for?"

A twinge of guilt erupts over his face. Everett knows I've got his number, and I'm petrified that I ever gave him mine.

Noah crops up and saves both Everett and me from any further hostile aggression.

"What's going on?" Noah looks to the two of us with an affable smile, and I suddenly want to shake it right off his body.

"Where's the good detective?" I ask, looking past him and coming up empty of one redhead. "Off to interrogate the family, I suppose? She is a professional. I don't see why the funeral should be off-limits."

Noah's brows pinch together in the middle, forming a perfect V, and suddenly I'm hungry, but it isn't for food. "She left. It's not uncommon for a homicide detective to pay his or her final respects at a public memorial. Besides, you never know who might show up."

"Like you," I muse, pulling him in and dotting his lips with a kiss. "I was just telling Everett about my little house hunt this afternoon." I shoot a death ray over to the nosy judge. "I'm looking at two houses, and they happen to be side by side. You wouldn't know anyone in the market for a rental, would you?" If Everett knows what's good for him, he'll go along with it. When he promised he wouldn't tell a soul, that umbrella undoubtedly covered Noah. But in the event he needs a reminder, I covertly stomp my stiletto over his shoe.

"Yes," he says it curt and directed right to me. "I do know of a few people looking to relocate." He looks to Noah with a glaring grin. "Lottie was kind enough to invite me to tag along. I'm ready as soon as you are."

"Great." Noah glances around the vicinity. "My realtor gave me the combination to the lock boxes. Why don't I meet the two of you out front and we'll head on over?"

"Perfect," I say. "I walked from the bakery, so if I can catch a ride with one of you, that would be best."

Noah nods to his stepbrother in the way you do when you're about to have an altercation. "You'll ride with me," he says before gifting me a kiss and speeding off in the direction of daylight pouring in from the front.

"What are you doing?" I hiss to Everett as soon as we're alone.

"I collect payment prior to delivery of the goods. If you want me to go on some asinine undercover op, then you need to spill it, Lemon. I'm worried about you, and I don't like that feeling."

"Why? Because you've never worried about anyone else before?" I'm betting not. But it's sweet of him to venture into unchartered territories for me so soon into our questionable friendship.

"Because I'm frightened for you." It comes out kind, softer than any other words he's ever spoken to me. "I'll meet you out front." Everett takes off, and I stand there trying to process how I landed in a vat of boiling emotional oil and how Hunter Fisher ended up in a casket.

I step out into the straggling crowd and note a woman hunched over near the front. She looks about my age, for sure a romantic contender as far as Hunter was concerned. A young man about the same age wraps his arms around her in an effort to comfort her. Although, judging by the way she's batting him away, she looks far more hostile than she ever does grieving. But that man, there's something about that dark head of curly hair that seems more than vaguely familiar, and then it hits me.

"It's him," I say under my breath as I speed on over.

The girl is pretty, long, dark, wavy hair and long, thick lashes that are most likely not from nature, but she's able to pull it off. Her lips are painted a bold shade of red-blue that my mother keeps trying to push on me, but I've tried it and, believe me when I say, it just makes me look like a clown, and a scary one at that. There's something theatrical about the girl in general, like she just stepped off a runaway to attend the funeral.

I hasten my way over, clearing my throat as I close in on them. "Excuse me," I say as I step in close. "I remember you," I say to the young man, and his expression irons out. "The bakery. You saved my life about a week ago. The scaffolding?"

He ticks his head back. "That's right. That was a close call. I'd say it was your lucky day." His skin is slightly pocked around his cheeks, and he's got a tattoo on his neck of a bird in flight that I didn't notice before.

"Well, it wasn't really. Hunter was gunned down behind my shop later that night. So it was a terrible day, actually."

The girl looks to her phone and flicks on her sunglasses. "I gotta run." She pushes past the crowd without so much as a goodbye.

"I'd better get her home. Glad to see you're safe." He takes off after her, and I'm left in their wake.

"But I didn't get your name!" I shout and suddenly feel like an idiot. I don't need his name. Most superheroes prefer it that way.

Everett and that first encounter we had come back to mind, and a quiet laugh bubbles from me.

He's going to be my superhero, all right, and Noah isn't going to know a thing about it.

BOBBING FOR BODIES

Country Cottage Road is just as cozy as its moniker implies. The streets are narrow and heavily lined with liquidambars and oaks in every spectrum of the citrine fall color spectrum. Each house has a cluster of pumpkins festooning its porch, and wreaths filled with fall leaves and acorns sit proudly against each and every door.

Noah parks in front of two gorgeous homes, one with white siding and a wraparound picket fence porch and the other a blue split-level with a balcony off the second story just above the front doors.

I take a step toward the white house and fall immediately in love with its bright red entry. "That *door*!" I coo. "And the banisters on the porch railing make it look as if it has a white picket fence. I think there's a clear winner."

Everett scowls at my quick assessment. "The only practical thing to do is look at both of them."

"That's just the logical side of you speaking," I say as I look across the street. "So, which one is yours?" I ask, threading an arm around Noah's waist.

"Second from the left." He points to the cabin-like home adjacent to the one I like.

"Perfect. I'll set my binoculars to look right into your living room window. I am prone to spy on occasion. I can't help it. It's the investigator in me." I give his side a quick pinch, and he laughs.

"Why do you think I brought these to your attention?" He waggles his brows. "I'm prone to do the same. I can't help it. It's the investigator in me."

We share a warm laugh before heading up to the white house, and Noah punches the combination to the lock box to let us inside. Immediately I'm taken.

"I am head over heels instantly in love," I say. "And that's my logical side speaking, Everett." I skip right out into the spacious living room with a custom cutout in the wall for a television that could fit the one I own perfectly. A large fireplace sits underneath with a stone hearth, and the room opens nicely to a decent-sized dining room. Then there is the pièce de résistance, a spacious kitchen with light granite countertops with enough white glazed cabinets to house everything I own in, an island with a genuine slab of white marble, and behind it sits a commercial grade high-end oven. "Where do I sign?"

Noah rumbles with a laugh. "Let's check out the bedrooms and make sure it's exactly what you want."

"Are you kidding?" Everett balks. "She's not signing anything until she thoroughly investigates option two. Never sell out before you have to, Lemon."

"I'm not selling out." I'm quick to roll my eyes. But, my God, how I would sell out in a second if I had that contract in front of me. Noah already ran the numbers past me on the way over, and both are within my reach.

We sail from room to room, and each inch of this cavernous well-lit place screams home to me.

"Pancake is going to love this place. There's so much for him to explore, to see, to do!"

"Pancake?" Everett looks as if I'm about to divulge the news of yet another supernatural wonder.

"Her cat," Noah is quick to divulge.

"My friend. My very *best* friend. But don't tell Keelie I said that. Pancake has been the dutiful man by my side ever since I brought him home." I shoot a quick look to Noah, hoping he might offer up his services in that department. I'm not looking for a proposal for Pete's sake. Just something to affirm how he feels about me.

"He sounds lovely," Everett says, pointing the way to the door. "Shall we inspect house number two?"

The three of us head over, and I'm pleasantly surprised to see a far more spacious home than the one we just left, with an extra bedroom and bathroom attached.

"It's amazing."

"Told you." Everett rocks back on his heels. "Always keep your options open, Lemon. You never know when you might be standing next to something better than what you have in hand."

Noah growls as if he were rabid. "What's that supposed to mean?"

"It means exactly what it says." He cuts him a sharp look. "I'm taking off. Thanks for letting me tag along for the adventure." He nods my way. "Lemon, text me when you're ready to claim your prize."

My mouth falls open as he strides out the door, and I'm fuming he left us with such a cryptic remark.

Noah ticks his head to the side. "Prize?"

My mouth opens once again, and I beg for anything to stream out of it. I'd settle for a not-so-white lie at this point.

"*Coffee.*" I shrug. "He bet I couldn't go through the funeral without bawling like a baby, and I managed to hold it together well enough, so he owes me coffee."

Noah inches back at the thought. "That's a terrible bet." He wraps his arms around me, and I rock steady in his arms.

"Everett's a terrible person." I'm only half-teasing at this point.

He belts out a laugh. "Go easy on him. He's only rough around the edges because he was raised to be."

It never occurred to me that Everett's tough persona was something inbred into him.

"Fair enough. I guess you're looking at your new neighbor. How fast do you think I can get the keys?"

"I'll talk to my realtor and find out asap. But let me be the first to welcome you to the neighborhood." He lands a heated kiss to my lips, and a moan works its way up my throat.

I pull back, nibbling on his lower lip playfully. "I'm thinking about hosting a housewarming party once I settle in, but since I'm on a strict budget, I'm only able to invite one person. Any idea who that should be?"

A dark laugh rumbles from him as he presses me against his chest. "I have an idea." His lids hood as he gets that naughty look in his eyes, and then just like that, he looks suddenly downcast. "But I have to ask. Are you and Everett hiding something from me?"

"No, not at all. I promise. It's not like that."

Did I just lie to Noah's face? Oh my God, this is all Everett Baxter's fault. If I lose the one good thing that's happened to me in a long time—aside from the bakery, of course—I'm going to wring Judge Baxter's illegally gorgeous neck.

"Good." He touches his forehead to mine. "Because I think we should start things off with open communication and one hundred percent honesty."

"Start things? Are we starting something?"

His eyes bear hard into mine, and my stomach does that roller coaster thing that makes me feel about thirteen-years-old again.

A crooked grin breaks out over his devilishly handsome face. "I think we've already begun."

"I think we have, too."

Noah crashes his lips to mine, and we indulge in a kiss far more daring than any of those shared before. Noah rides his arms up and down my back, along my hips before securing me tight in a warm embrace. Noah and I have started something. We are at the beginning of something that I predict will be spectacularly beautiful.

Noah wants open communication and one hundred percent honesty.

I can't help but sigh as I indulge in everything he's willing to give me.

One out of two isn't bad.

11

It turns out, Martinelle Finance isn't located in your routine run-of-the-mill bank, nor is it located in an offshoot due to the fact the loans department is under construction. As fate, a heck of a lot of googling, and utilizing Everett's connections would have it—the two of us find ourselves seated in a holding room that happens to be in an underground gambling casino hidden behind your average strip club—if indeed the scandalous venue Everett and I walked through to get here was average. That's yet to be determined, and not by me. I held Everett's hand the entire time we were whisked through the place, and as soon as the bras came off those heavily made up dancing girls, I closed my eyes and let Everett lead me blindly through that den of depravity. Red Satin is a dicey establishment that I never want to set foot in again, let alone have an entire string of catcalls shouted at me as I strutted my way through it. Although, in hindsight, those catcalls were most likely for the topless girls dancing for their dinner.

"We're going to get shot," I whisper directly into Everett's ear.

He pulls back and rolls his eyes as if it were an asinine thought while a man in a white suit clicks away at a computer monitor in front of us.

If this seedy locale, and this dizzying cube of a room they've stuffed us in, didn't ring any alarms, then his glaring fashion faux pas should have sent us running.

The heavyset man seated in front of us chokes on a cough. His nose sits crooked on his face as if it were broken at one time and someone didn't set it right. "You're in luck, Mr. and Mrs. Essex. We've got a special lending program for folks such as yourself."

Yourself. That fake grin on my face expands once he lets that grammar offense fly.

I give Everett's hand a firm squeeze, and he gives a slight squeeze back. And in no way and at no time did it feel at all sexual holding Everett's hand—more like self-preservation. I'm sure Noah would forgive me if he knew the circumstances. And yet, Noah can never ever know the circumstances—which, of course, completely dismantles all that whole open communication and one hundred percent honesty clause we hammered out the other night. But there are simply some things that need to be done for the greater good of the people—even if that particular person is dead. Hunter needed justice, and I'm not sitting on my hands—or baking a cake as Noah would have it—until Ivy Fairbanks decides she's going to solve this mystery.

"What are the terms?" Everett leans in, that serious expression still pinned on his face. He decided to eschew my fashion advice and wore a suit anyhow. And now that we're in this hot box, I don't mind at all that Everett looks so intimidating.

The man in the white suit twirls the pencil in his hand while staring Everett down. There is definitely some male testosterone showdown going on that I want no part in. Thank God I dragged Everett down here with me. I can't imagine how terrifying this entire experience would have been if it were just my butter knife and me. I really do need to up my game in the weapons department. The least I can do is carry around a bottle of pan spray so I can blind a perpetrator or two.

"Now"—Mr. White Suit tosses his hands over his desk—"in no way am I a loan shark. This is a short-term small industry loan."

"Numbers," Everett grumbles. "I need numbers."

"Okay, okay. I'll give you the full amount due on signing. Ten points for a six-month window with each month compounding. In other words, it would behoove you to pay it off in a month." He blinks a quick smile. "It would behoove me for you to pay it back in six months or never—collateral being the house once you sign. Until then, I'll hold the spare keys to the two a yous vehicles. You can bring those in when we do the exchange."

I lean in and clear my throat. "How fast can we get the money?"

His chest bucks a few times with a dry laugh. "Honey, I got the money here today. Getting the money isn't a problem. You'll have your bank account filled legally. We write cashier's checks. And lastly, we do a drive-by twice a week past your residence. Consider it an added layer of security you didn't know you needed."

"We won't skip town," Everett notes, and I jump in my seat.

My God, I didn't even connect the mafia-inspired dots! And here I thought these nice men were looking to keep our shiny new neighborhood crime-free. Ha! And *they're* the criminals!

My entire body heats to unsafe levels, and suddenly I'm itching to get out of here. But what about Hunter?

I glance around and spot a file cabinet that looks rusted shut, then another quick sweep for any evidence of security camera and an idea comes to me. That computer he's tap-dancing on is my best bet.

"Excuse me"—I lift a finger weakly as I interject—"would you mind giving us a moment together so we can process this? It's a lot to take in and uh..." Boss Hog here looks as if his patience with me is dwindling. "Well, I'm just a little ol' baker, and I need my big, strong husband to translate all those daunting numbers for me." As if. I shed a wide smile. That was one lie I didn't mind at all imparting.

He gives a sober shake of the head. "Oh, I get it."

And I figured you would.

He struggles to rise before hitting the door. "I'm gonna run next door and grab a cold one. Can I get you anything?"

Both Everett and I decline his offer. No sooner does the door shut behind him than I bolt over and seal my body against it.

"What are you doing?" Everett hisses, his eyes bulging with horror.

"I'm shielding the door while you look for any files on Hunter Fisher on that computer!"

"Geez." Everett looks as if I've just threatened to run over him with a semi. "I'll hold the door. I am not violating anybody's privacy. I happen to make a living off of other people trampling over one another's constitutional rights."

He trades places with me, and I bolt to the desk where a screensaver of a scantily clad woman with her thighs split open jars me before I hit a key and the dashboard loads before me. I click into finder and begin scanning for anything that might remotely get me to where I want to be. There's a file marked *Open Cases*, and I quickly scan an entire roster of names, only to realize there's enough to fill a phonebook.

"I'll never get to the end of this," I hiss.

"Get to the end of it now," Everett hisses back. "I'm giving you less than thirty seconds to get back in your seat."

"Fine." I shut the file down and note one with the name *Closed Cases*. "Maybe it's here."

There's a rustle outside the door, and both Everett and I freeze solid. Everett is glaring at me as if I had accidentally dragged him off to ground zero just before a nuclear warhead were to drop out of the sky. And, honestly, that might have been more painless. The rustling subsides, and I get back to clicking. My entire body breaks out into a sweat. I can hardly steady my breathing as I scan the list all the way to the letter F.

"Hunter Fisher!" I practically screech his name out.

"*Sshh*," Everett hushes me just as loud.

"Okay, let's see what it says." I whip my phone out and snap a few pictures of the screen before reading over it quickly. "Two loans for the amount of three thousand dollars each. Both paid off in full. Ten points on pick up. March of last year and July. The foot note says—" I scan over it myself and can hardly believe it.

"What does it say?" Everett flicks his hand through the air, signaling for me to speed it up.

"It says money for girlfriend. Money for kid." Huh.

The sound of a belly laugh coming from down the hall proceeds to get louder, and I'm betting it's Mr. White Suit.

I quickly shut down the file, and both Everett and I slide back into our seats.

The door swings open. "So, what's it gonna be, kids? You in?"

"On second thought"—I rise out of my chair as does Everett—"I'm going to ask my mother one more time."

Everett nods. "But if she says no, we're coming right back. Believe me, she's the last person I want to deal with."

Mr. White Suit laughs it up before giving Everett a commiserating slap to the back. "Sounds good. Go get yourself something good to eat. I've got a pastrami sandwich in the microwave. You let yourselves out." He leaves the door open as he takes off, and I spontaneously wrap my arms around Everett.

"Way to go, Mr. Sexy. You really lived up to your name." I pull back to get a better look at him. "Hey, if I didn't know better, I'd say you were blushing."

"I'm not. It's about two hundred degrees in here. We literally sweated this one out." He presses his hand into the small of my back as he ushers us to the door. "But I think we make a heck of a team, Lemon."

"I know we do. And we make a pretty cute couple, too. You were brilliant. I could just kiss you."

We share a laugh before speeding our way through the strip club. Everett tries to turn his head toward the stage, and I don't hesitate to swat him.

As soon as we hit daylight, we hightail it to the fast food restaurant across the street where Everett parked his car. I met him at the coffee shop in Ashford as planned, and once we get back, I plan on caffeinating myself back to the land of the living after that near-death experience with the underworld.

"What do you say we blow this one cow town and I buy you a cup a joe, Mr. Sexy?" I tease. Way back when he refused to give me his name, I hung out at the coffee counter and snooped to see what the barista would scrawl onto his cup. It turns out, she had the aforementioned hot-to-trot moniker picked out just for him.

"Mr. Sexy?" a female voice bleats from behind, and we turn to find a haughty redhead tucked in a black pea coat.

"Detective Fairbanks." I'm so stunned to see her I keep blinking in hopes she'll evaporate like a bad vision.

She ticks her head to the side with a husky laugh. "Heard it all. The two of you really do make a cute couple."

My mouth falls open. "You did hear it all, didn't you?"

She strides our way, her affect hard as flint. "It's called surveillance, sweetie. The place is tapped. The entire conversation was on blast."

A thousand scenarios run through my head at once, and all of them involve Noah. The world sways beneath my feet, and I can hardly catch my next breath.

"I swear it's not what it looks like. You can't tell Noah."

A shadowed figure steps out from behind her, and into the light emerges Noah Corbin Fox.

"She doesn't have to tell me, Lottie." His voice is calm yet strained. "I heard every last word."

GAH!

He didn't hear the part about Mr. Sexy, did he? Because I totally did not mean that. It's simply a fact that baristas the world over most likely agree upon.

"Noah..." I try to take a step in his direction, but my toes feel as if they've screwed themselves into the ground. "I'm so sorry. I—"

"Don't." He holds up a hand and glares at Everett. "You took her right into the armpit of danger. You could have gotten yourselves killed," he growls out the words as the cords in his neck distend. Noah charges at Everett and slams him against his SUV before I can process any of it.

"*Whoa!*" Ivy Fairbanks riots and does her best to pluck Noah right off. "You do not get to screw up my investigation. I'm taking you off the case, Fox." Her icy stare never leaves his. "And if I see any of you diving back into it, I'll have you all arrested." She glares over at Everett. "I expected more out of you." She looks to Noah. "I'll give you a lift back to the station if you need it."

"I accept," he says, his hard gaze still penetrating mine.

We watch as Ivy Fairbanks and Noah disappear around the corner, and it feels as if my chest implodes, crushing my heart completely.

"I've ruined everything," I whisper, my entire body numb to the world. "It's over."

Something tells me, Noah and I will never recover.

12

Days drone by, and no matter how much I text, visit his office, or stalk at his house, Noah Fox always has a seemingly good reason why we can't meet up.

Apparently, his cases have given birth to baby cases, and he's up all night with those, too. He doesn't have a free moment to spare for me it seems. I can't blame him. Here he was giving me the best his lips had to offer and how did I repay him? By doing exactly what he kindly asked me not to do—with his sexy stepbrother no less.

Darn Everett for having such an adorable and frighteningly accurate moniker. Not that this is all Everett's fault. As it turns out, he's not so pleased with me either. Everett has been busy these past few days, too, and for that I'm feeling thankful. I'm also thankful that the bakery has been filled to the brim at all hours of every day. At least this way I'm too busy baking up a storm and eating my feelings to digest what a dumpster fire I've managed to turn my life into.

An ear-piercing cackle comes from the large group near the window. Apparently, Naomi Turner has started up a naughty book club for the pre-menopausal—her word choice, not mine, and the who's who of said non-hormonally challenged age bracket is all present and accounted for.

Lily Swanson, Naomi's mean and bitter bestie, sits dutifully by her left side. And ensconcing the queen of mean on her right is my bestie, Keelie, who apologized through the roof for not getting their sleazy read to me in time to participate. But she did politely point out that while they were doling out the bawdy book, I was up to my eyeballs trying to solve poor Merilee's murder last month. Speaking of Merilee, her cousin, Cascade, is here cackling right along with the rest of them. With that long, dark hair of hers and her penchant for crushed velvet, she seems to be carrying on the legacy of the Simonson sisters nicely. Ellen Rawlings from the bank showed up. She hasn't stopped showing off those illuminated teeth of hers since she sat down. Funny, I've never once seen her smile during our banal monetary transactions. Nice to know she's capable. Darlene Grand, whose family owns the apple orchard, and Janet Darren, Travis Darren's lookalike sister, sit attentively as if there will be a quiz later—and knowing Naomi, and her need for dominance, there might be. Travis Darren was the one dating Merilee and Mora Anne at the very same time—thus driving Mora Anne to the brink of insanity. He's basically the primary reason Merilee was stabbed to death by her sister. Some men are heartbreakers. Travis was quite literally a heart taker in a roundabout way.

Collette Jenner shoots me a sharp look from over her shoulder, and I can't help but snarl at her slightly. Collette can't seem to keep her paws off of her legal eagle ex, and, yet, Everett has said a thousand times he's not interested in pursuing anything romantic with her again. Some people just can't take the hint. Speaking of which, it reminds me. I need to text Noah again at some point today. You never know when his schedule will free up.

Lainey waves me over, and I can't help but think she's a little traitor. I'll admit, it stung a bit not to be included on this innovated literary effort that just about every woman from Honey Hollow in my age group seems to be a part of. I grab my carafe and head on over. Lainey is seated next to Molly McMurry, so I'll hold any snippy comments for later.

I'm still blown away by the fact Molly wants me to provide all the cupcakes for the Fall-O-Ween event next week, and the last thing I want is for her to see me sporting a bad attitude.

"More coffee, ladies?" I hold up my carafe, but they're all too engrossed in the steamy passage they're dissecting to notice me, so I do a quick round of refills anyhow.

The bell tied to the door chimes and in breezes a pale Micheline Roycroft with her copy of *Fit to be Tied* in her hand as she breezes to the seat next to my sister.

"Did I miss anything?" Her entire face brightens as she smiles up at me. I'd swear her smile just warmed the whole place. The last few times I've seen Micheline she's looked miserable beyond recognition. I guess she's coming to terms with Hunter's death, as she should.

I shake my head. "I don't know. But they've been here for an hour and there have been lots of spontaneous outbursts of—" I'm about to say *laughter* just when the room explodes with wild cackles once again.

Chrissy Nash and Eve Hollister amble in and give the younger sect the stink eye.

I head over and take their orders, two lattes, two chocolate-filled croissants, an order that's quickly becoming their usual.

Eve leans over to Chrissy. Eve's salt and peppered curls are certainly looking more salt these days than pepper. "I suppose our blood pressure is too high to be a part of that club," she huffs, indignant.

Chrissy, a fit blonde whom the mayor dumped because, well, let's face it, he's an idiot, chortles away. "I'm guessing you're right. I guess it's a good thing that our book club meets at the B&B this month." She looks my way. "Your mother is hosting a haunted high tea."

"Sounds delightful." I know all about it because my mother has put me in charge of providing all the petit fours for the aforementioned event. "And what book will you ladies be reading? A steamy historical romance, perhaps?"

Eve smirks as she waves me off. "You know us all too well, Lottie. *The Duke's Haunted Bedchamber* has been steaming up my glasses for weeks."

Chrissy's mouth falls open. "Since when does it take you weeks to finish a book?"

"It doesn't. I'm on my third go-round. Some books are so hauntingly delish they deserve a reread or two. Besides, with my house in shambles, I've nothing better to do than read by the fire."

"Still working on the remodel?" I ask. It's a well-known fact that Eve Hollister's retrofitting of her mansion has been going on for a small eternity.

"There's no end to it, Lottie. For the love of all that is holy, do not invest in a fixer."

A dull laugh thumps in my chest. A fixer to Eve would be a model home to most.

I hand them their coffee and croissants and sigh dreamily at that house across from Noah's with its white picket railing. I haven't heard word back, but a part of me wonders if Noah has told the realtor to forget it. There's no way he wants to live in close proximity to me after that fiasco down in Leeds. Face it, I'm the fiasco he wants no part of.

The book club concludes, and all dozen or so of them stand at once.

Naomi claps the murmuring crowd back into submission. "The next book we're reading is *The Thankful Subservient*. I think it will tie in nicely with Thanksgiving."

"Get it? *Tie* in?" Lily guffaws right in her bestie's face, but Naomi is quick to brush her off.

Collette Jenner pulls on a black pea coat, and her bright orange curls cascade off the back. The black and orange give off a Halloween vibe that I'm sure she wasn't going for, but she is scary. I'll give her that.

"You never let us pick our next read. We should take it to a vote." Collette dares defy the head witch of this unholy coven.

But Naomi doesn't flinch. "We don't need a vote. The books I pick are fantastic. Did I let anyone down with this month's selection?"

A round of approving giggles circles the small crowd before it officially disbands.

I waste no time in picking up a platter of fresh oatmeal cookies with adorable iced spider webs over the tops and head over to Micheline, but Lily Swanson gets in my way.

"The sign in the front says you're hiring, and I want in." Her large, glossy, green eyes look as if they're about to pop with anticipation. "Rumor has it, that hot judge keeps hanging around. And, seeing that I'm newly single"—so another rumor is true, she's up and dumped Travis—"I can use a handsome man with a hefty paycheck."

I can't help but frown. I'm about to shut down the gold digger in front of me when—although I have no doubt she's attracted to Everett—she is right, he is a rather hot commodity—Keelie bubbles her way over.

"Yes!" Keelie threads her arm through Lily's. "The bakery is running off fumes from the Honey Pot, and we so need our staff back. Can you bake?"

Lily shudders as if the concept offended her. "No, but I can run a register like it's nobody's business."

"You're hired." Keelie doesn't waste a moment as she whisks her away. "I just need you to fill out an application, and then I'll assign you some hours."

So much for discerning the right people to populate the bakery with.

Micheline whips on her jacket, and I quickly dash in front of her before she has the chance to leave. I just have to know if she's aware of any girlfriend Hunter might have had who happened to be a mother. I've been racking my brain trying to think of anyone in Honey Hollow who fits the description but come up with blanks.

"Oatmeal cookie?" I hold the platter in front of her, and she's quickly overcome by the heavy scent of cinnamon and vanilla.

"My God, these smell divine." She snaps one off the tray and indulges in a moaning bite. "So good. I'd say you really should sell these, but you beat me to it." A tiny dimple imbeds itself into her cheek as she grins.

As much as I loathe to ruin her good mood, Hunter's murder investigation is growing colder by the moment, so I dive right in. "Hey, I heard a funny rumor about Hunter, and I wondered if you heard it, too." I wrinkle my nose while playing up the chagrinned angle. "Was he dating someone with a kid? I mean, it's no big deal, but Hunter and I were pretty close, and he's always liked kids, so I wondered why he never mentioned it."

Her naturally pasty complexion turns a bright shade of pomegranate, and I can't help but think I've stumbled upon something big. Either that or I've just shocked her so badly there won't be enough spider web iced oatmeal cookies in the world to revive her.

"He"—a croaking sound emits from her throat as if she were deciding which lane she wanted to get into—"he was seeing someone." She closes her eyes a moment and shakes her head as if she couldn't believe she had to go there—as if she couldn't believe *he* had to go there. "It was stupid. Some stripper from Leeds."

I suck in a quick breath, trying my best to think on my feet. "The one from Red Satin?" *Brill!* Suddenly, I'm thankful for my minute knowledge of all things scantily clad.

"No"—she bats her eyes to the ceiling as if trying to remember the name and, dear God, I pray she remembers the name—"it was Girls Unlimited." Her lips purse with disgust. "Anyway, that was a bigger deal than he intended it to be. You might even say it was the nail in our casket." She winces. "Sorry. I don't mean to be disrespectful." Micheline's whole affect shifts, and suddenly she looks crestfallen. "I'd better get going." She snaps another cookie off the tray. "Thanks for being such a good friend, Lottie."

"No problem." A good friend who pumps a grieving girl for info. Some good friend I am.

Lainey comes up, and I manufacture a smile for my sister. "Are you free tonight?"

"Yeah, why?" Her brows dip as she sinks her suspicion my way.

"You might want to let your hair down and leave your reading glasses at home. We're headed to a strip club in Leeds."

Naomi and Collette Jenner scuttle over with their eyes agog.

"I'm in." Naomi doesn't miss a topless beat.

"Me, too," Collette gruffs it out as if she's angry about it before stalking to the door. "Naomi, text me with the details. I've got a board meeting all afternoon, and God knows I'll need to unwind." A salacious grin rides up her cheeks. "I'm all for an appetizer before I sink my teeth into Judge Baxter's neck." She bares her fangs as she speeds into the chilled autumn air.

"She's quite the vampire," Lainey notes. "So, what's with the strip club? Two men not enough for you, lady?" She shakes her shoulders in a suggestive manner. Good Lord, Lainey really is in training to become my mother.

Keelie shuffles over, nearly tripping over a chair. "Did someone say strip club? Dear God up in heaven, you are not going without me. You'll need a tour guide who speaks the language and knows where to put the dollar bills!"

Lainey chortles. "I didn't know you speak banana hammock?"

The three of them share a titillating laugh.

Little do they know there won't be a banana hammock in sight at Girls Unlimited. I may not know which stripper Hunter dated, but I do know she's got a kid. That should narrow the field significantly.

I have a feeling I'm about to split this case wide open with a stripper pole.

Noah bounces through my mind. I know for a fact he wouldn't want me digging back into the investigation, but then we're technically not speaking so he doesn't really have a say.

Keelie and Naomi screech with laughter at something Lainey says, and I cringe.

Something tells me Girls Unlimited will be one banana hammock short of what they're looking for.

13

"What do you mean every stripper in here has a kid?" I shout above the music to the bartender I've enlisted to help me find Hunter's mystery girl.

I shoot a quick glance to Lainey, Naomi, Keelie, and Collette who sulk at a table nearby. Not one of them is hooting and hollering at deafening decibels the way they threatened to on the way over. Suffice it to say, I'll have to bake a batch of banana hammock muffins just to get back in their good graces.

"That's what I said." The bald and brawny bartender tatted from the neck down continues cleaning out a glass with a dishrag. It's so dimly lit in this seedy establishment, save for the stage where the girls working hard for a dollar have an entire bevy of spotlights dancing around them. "They've all got kids. What else you got on her?"

Crap. The music is so loud it sounds as if a jet engine has suddenly decided to spit out rap tunes. Although, I'm slightly grateful for the scent of fries permeating the air. The first thing I did when we got seated was order a round for the table. Who knew they served appetizers here? *Hey*? Maybe I can work out a deal for weekly cookie deliveries? But, at the moment, I'm coming up short on what cookie goes best with beer.

"She was dating someone who works construction," I add.

He shakes his head, that dead look on his face lets me know I've hit another bump in the road with far too many options to choose from.

"He was from Honey Hollow," I shout the words just as the music hits a lull, and someone from the back whoops *Honey Hollow* right back.

The bartender's mouth opens as he cocks a squinted eye to the ceiling. "Yeah, I know of one."

Lainey comes up and gives my sleeve a quick tug. "The girls and I want to go. We gave you your five minutes, and they were up ten minutes ago. Collette is threatening me with kidnapping if I don't get back on the road soon."

I avert my eyes at the thought. I knew bringing Collette and Naomi along would be a big mistake, but then I reasoned it might work out if we were surrounded with a tough crowd. That way we'd have someone to feed them while the rest of us made our escape. Besides, Naomi and Collette have the power to scare off any thug who has the nerve to mess with us.

"Five more minutes, I swear. I'm just getting to the good part!" I hiss before turning back to my tatted-up friend. "What's the girl's name?"

"Stella." He nods to the stage. "That's her up front."

My heart thumps wildly in my chest as I spin on my heels. There are at least six women on stage, each one wiggling and jiggling to the soothing sounds of a slow song that's currently melting over the speakers. The girls all look too beautiful to be real with their long, glossy hair, their showy curves, those sparkly pasties catching the light and arresting our vision. Then I see her. A woman with long, dark, wavy hair and long, thick lashes, and a familiar deep red lipstick that makes me suck in a lungful of stale French fried scented air.

"It's *her*," I hiss, and Lainey pulls me over to our table.

"Her who?"

"The girl from Hunter's funeral. I think I just found out who Hunter's mystery girlfriend was."

"Which one?" Naomi looks bored as she stares at the scandalous show before us.

"The girl up front—dark hair, purple pasties." I guess I do have a lot to be thankful for when I realize that no one will ever point me out in a crowd by way of the color of my nipple coverings.

"That's Sparkling Cider." Keelie gives a mean whoop her way. "You want me to make it rain over her? I've got some serious cash burning a hole in my pocket and not a lot of prospects."

"*No*," both Collette and I say at once.

I glance to the irate redhead who looks as if she's itching to bolt.

Collette sneers at Keelie. "Save the dinero. There's a place down the street called The Ladies Lounge and, trust me, there's not a purple pasty in the place. I wouldn't lead you astray, unlike some people." She takes a moment to glare my way. "And what would Everett think if he knew this was the kind of place you preferred to frequent?" Her lips twitch with a malevolent smile. "I'm pretty sure that would take you out of the running to fill his heart."

"Believe me, that man is not looking to fill his heart." It's yet to be determined that he has one. "And, fine, we'll leave—but not before I see the end of Sparkling Cider's act. As soon as she steps off that stage, I'm going to ask her a question."

I know for a fact once the girls are through they trot down and mingle with the masses. I'm betting those personal lap dances are where they make the real money. I can't imagine Hunter frequenting this place, but I know both he and Bear have amassed some serious frequent flyer miles at places just like this. For a second I envision Noah seated in some secluded booth and Sparkling Cider shaking her baby maker in his face. My stomach sours at the thought.

The girls finish up their tantalizing tease, leaving their G-strings and pasties right where they belong, and that alone makes me want to tip them. All six of them make their way down the stairs to the left of the stage, and a raucous rock song starts in and another set of temptresses in hot pink satin robes strut out as if they were about to teach us all a lesson.

"We're out," Naomi knocks back the rest of her drink before pulling Keelie to her feet.

Lainey and I stand, as does Collette, but Collette isn't putting on her coat just yet. She's grinning ear to ear at something behind me.

I turn my neck just enough before doing a double take.

"Oh God," I whimper under my breath. For the life of me I just can't catch a break.

Striding our way, shoulders back, clad in his signature sexy suit, those piercing blue eyes of his slotted to angry slits is a stone cold, chest wide as a linebacker judgmental Judge Baxter.

"*Everett.*" I try to sound cheery as if this were any other venue I might have bumped into him in. "You're looking grand tonight. Have a pocketful of Benjamins just begging for a pair of panties to stuff themselves into?" I couldn't help it. He so had it coming.

The good judge doesn't so much as a flinch. "What are you doing here, Lemon? When Collette mentioned you dragged her off to a strip club, I didn't believe her."

Collette wastes no time in snuggling up next to him, doing the worm over the left side of his body, but Everett doesn't even notice. "That's right. I sent him a picture of you loading up at the bar. Can you believe it?" She cackles into his ear. "Honey Hollows not-so-sweet baker showing her true colors. And, as it turns out, there's a *rainbow* involved."

"Oh stop." I lunge at her and she's quick to cower.

"All right." Lainey holds up a hand. "Let's get to The Ladies Lounge and banana hammock it up. It's almost my bedtime."

"I'm not going." I do a quick scan of the room and spot Sparkling Cider bouncing on the lap of some mussed hair businessman. "There's someone I need to talk to. I have unfinished business, and I'm getting to the bottom of it." My God, this might just be the most unhygienic conversation I've had with a person yet.

"I'll be with her." Everett nods to Lainey. "And I'll give her a ride back," he says it stern my way. And why does it sound like I'm about to be punished? "We have an unfinished conversation of our own we need to tend to."

My entire body seizes. I'm not sure which is worse: grilling a stripper about her dead boyfriend or diving into the deep end of dead pets with Everett.

Lainey, Naomi, and a seething mad Collette pluck a whooping Keelie from climbing on stage and hit the door for far more testosterone-laden pastures.

It's just Everett and I glaring at one another.

The glint of a purple pasty hits my eye, and I gasp.

"Here she comes." I wave over at her, and she struts on over with those long doe eyelashes tipped with glitter, those ruby red lips looking at Everett as if she too were ready and willing to take a bite out of his neck.

She moans as she caresses his tie, "You need a lap dance, big boy?" She bites down on her lip while her just about naked girls smash over Everett's steely abs. And really? Why does this feel as if I'm in a bad nightmare that's about to get porny?

"Actually, it's me that called you here."

Gone in an instant is that gleam in her eye as she inspects me head to foot. "Fine. Take a seat on the chair."

I do as I'm told, and before I know it, her backside is bouncing in my face and I try my hardest to slap her away.

Everett averts his eyes as he helps the poor girl off.

"I don't think she really wants to play the bongos." His demeanor is downright serious as he pulls out a seat for the girl. "You're up, Lemon."

Sparkling Cider looks as if she's about to lose her effervescence and hightail it over to the bar, so I get right to the chase.

"Hunter Fisher has a message for you." My entire body spikes with heat at the lie.

Her mouth falls open, and she jumps in her seat. "But—but Hunter's dead."

Ah-ha! So she does know him!

"Yes, he is, unfortunately. But before he died, he asked me to give someone he was seeing at Girls Unlimited a message."

"That's me!" Her eyes expand to the size of silver dollars. "What is it? Am I in his will?"

My gut wrenches at the thought of poor Hunter having a will at such a young age.

"Um—" I glance to Everett, completely unaware of where to go next with this.

Everett takes in a deep breath, and she looks his way, practically drooling over how wide that man's chest can get in a single lungful.

"Hunter had a certificate of deposit made out for you, but it was damaged and it can't be replaced. His attorney offers his apologies but—"

"That stupid, *stupid* idiot. Screwing up finances right up until the end." Her eyes gloss over with tears, and as upset as I am that she was calling him names, I can tell she cared a lot about him. Or the money. It's debatable at this point.

"I agree." I shrug over at her. "Hunter was always broke, and I couldn't figure out why. He mentioned something about you having a kid. A boy, right?" Just a wild guess. The worst she could do is correct me, considering it's a fifty-fifty split.

Stella freezes stiff. Her eyes slit to nothing as she looks past me out into some unknowable horizon. "I prefer to leave my son out of this." The music dies down as the applause picks up and Stella rises out of her seat. "Besides, I don't need anything else from Hunter." She hightails it into the crowd before disappearing into the back.

"That was abrupt." Everett helps me out of my seat.

"I agree. You know that underground source you used to help us find Martinelle Finance? Do me a favor and have them find out everything there is to know about Sparkling Cider, aka Stella. I have a feeling that's not the last we'll see of her yet."

"Will do," he says as he steps in close. That towering presence of his makes me feel about as big as a shoe. "But first, you're going to tell me all there is to know about you."

I take a deep, exasperating breath, girding myself for the inevitable.

"I guess my moment of reckoning has finally come."

"That it has, Lemon."

Everett presses his hand against my back as he navigates us out of the seedy club, and I can't help but think I'm walking to my doom. And in a way, I am.

I'd rather trade places with Hunter than try to explain my supernatural superpowers with someone as logically minded as Everett.

This will not end well.

But I'm guessing it will be the end of our friendship.

14

The McMurry Pumpkin Patch gleams like a crown filled with amber jewels on this late October night. Everett offered to take us out for something warm to drink, and I opted for cider. There seems to be a theme tonight. And Everett, being the gentleman he is, opted to hold off our chat until we each had a warm cup in our hands.

The moon shines down from the east, casting long shadows across the fields laden with enough pumpkins to create a pie for every person in North America. We settle on a couple of bales of hay and look out at all of the families enjoying the festivities. There are pumpkin carving stations, three oversized bounce houses sagging and rocking in rhythm, and a petting zoo filled to capacity with both humans and animals—and the sight of the furry creatures sours my expression because it's a harsh reminder of why we're here.

"So I've done some research"—Everett begins—"within the community of people who believe in those kind of afterlife phenomena. Seeing dead pets is not entirely uncommon."

I make a face at his attempt to put a quasi-scientific spin on things. "And what's your verdict? Are you going to lock me up in a psychiatric facility for life, or do I get the electric chair?"

"Neither." His shoulders sag as he scoots in another inch. "Tell me your history. When did this begin? What exactly *is* this?"

My eyes close involuntarily as I try to summon the right words, in the right order, but they won't come.

"Okay, I'm just going to blurt this out." I take a quick breath, my gaze pinned to those blue flames that are ready to torch my world down. "When I was a kid, I started seeing creatures that happen to be missing a tangible body—little see-through cute and furry ghosts, if you will." I sigh at how ridiculous it sounds coming from my lips. "Anyway, one day I saw a little turtle floating near Bear's ear, and later that afternoon he broke his arm. So the next time I saw a little disembodied beast, I held my breath and, sure enough, it happened again—and again, and again, and again. And then, of course, there was Merilee's orange Tabby, which I saw on the same day I met you. That was the first time anyone actually bit the big one. But now that I think on it, everything that's ever transpired has been pretty awful."

He ticks his head back, just trying to absorb it all. "How about your family, your mother, your father? Do they share the same gift?"

"I was adopted by the Lemons when I was just an infant. There's no telling who my real family is. Like I mentioned before, the only other person on the planet who's aware of this is Nell Sawyer. She's my best friend, Keelie's, grandmother, and well, mine by proxy. She didn't judge me." I glance out to the pumpkin patch for a moment as a truck filled with bales of hay and a happy load of passengers goes by. "But you'll judge me." It comes out lower than a whisper. "You can't help it. It's what you do for a living."

"I don't judge like that." He bounces his hand over mine a moment. "Lemon, as strange as it sounds, I believe you. I don't claim to understand everything about this universe. And if that's what you say happens, then I accept that as the truth. And I can tell that you're telling the truth.

I'd like to ask your forgiveness for prying. I just needed to be clear that in no way this would've impeded on the case."

"And what have you decided?" I'm almost teasing, but you never know with Everett.

"You're in the clear." He takes a sip of his cider. "You want me to take you home?"

"Actually, now that you know all about my family history, I was hoping you could share something about your own. Noah mentioned that his father took your mother to the cleaners. I feel just terrible about that—especially since I ended up turning her misfortune into appliances for the bakery."

Everett pumps out a dull laugh. "Well, he didn't exactly clean her out. He did, however, put in a darn good effort. Despite the fact, my mother is still a wealthy woman. She still lives in Fallbrook. Still cautiously single. She's a hotel heiress. My grandfather owned a chain of five-star hotels across Europe. I've got a sister, Meghan. She works for an insurance company. She's still back in Fallbrook as well. Single, no pets." He smirks over at me, and I pretend to sock him on the arm.

"And you?" I lift a shoulder his way as if I were being coy. "How are you possibly single? I mean, I get that whole exes thing. I've met them. But why haven't you settled down yet?"

Everett turns toward the fields and takes a deep breath. "Guess I haven't found the one."

"You will. You'll be off the market soon enough, believe me. And there will be a body count, too. Women are going to war over you."

He winces. "Coming from you, the body count sounds like a threat."

"Sadly, coming from me, it might be."

"And you?" He touches his shoulder to mine as if to prod me. "Are you off the market?"

My stomach sinks because I can't seem to find the answer. "I thought I was. Noah and I seemed to be going pretty strong. I just—he never told me how he felt about me, and I was left questioning whether or not he wanted something exclusive with me."

"Did you want something exclusive with him?" He bears those ocean blue eyes into mine, and a shiver runs through me.

"Yes, I wanted it. I mean, Noah's a great guy. He just— I don't know. He doesn't want me tampering in what he refers to as his investigation. And I get that to a certain extent. But Hunter was my friend. I can't just let it go and hope for the best. There's a bona fide killer out there. And if he or she isn't caught soon, they might just strike again."

"I get that. But I also get where Noah is coming from. You're a great person, Lemon. And at the risk of losing a friendship, I have to say I agree with him. He doesn't want to see you get hurt and neither do I. I'm sorry, but it's safety first. You said it yourself. There's a bona fide killer out there who might be looking for another victim. We don't want that to be you."

"Neither do I." I sag into the words. "I don't really fault Noah for wanting to keep me safe. Or you." I knock my knee into his as an entire gaggle of kids run for the pick-up area for the next round of hayrides. "Say, you wouldn't happen to know if Noah has any hang-ups about relationships, would you?"

He cocks his head to the side. "I know his ex was a pistol. I'm sure that made him more than a little cautious. But that's his story to tell. If he's smart, he'll commit to you soon. He's not a player anymore."

"A player, huh?" I can't help but giggle at the thought. "Did you take the baton from him?"

He groans as he cringes. "I might have taken a page out of his playbook. Both he and his brother were a bad influence on me back in the day." He glowers toward the pumpkin patch as if he were having a bad memory. "You know what? How about we hop on that hayride real quick? It'll be a nice palate cleanse before we head on out."

"*Judge Baxter*." I laugh as I hop up and dust the hay from my jeans. "You really do know how to have a good time."

We finish up our cider and board the tractor-trailer, seating ourselves near the back, a safe distance from the howling masses. Everett and I laugh during every inch of that bumpy, twisted, and jerking good time. And once the tractor comes to a stop, we're the last to get off. Everett exits first. It's so murky and dark in this area of the pumpkin patch it all feels like a dream.

"This night sure took a turn for the—" I'm about to say *better* when my foot glides right off the hay bale that's acting as a stepladder and Everett catches me in his arms.

"*Whoa!*" he says as the momentum sends us spinning, and I laugh as we come to a complete stop just shy of the petting zoo.

"Looks like fun," a masculine voice calls out from behind, and Everett swings me back around, only to have my heart stop cold.

"*Noah?*" I squint into the darkness, hoping against hope it's just Ken, the owner, wanting to give me the final count on how many devil's food cupcakes to bake for the Fall-O-Ween Fest—but this is me we're talking about. That handsome brick wall of a man glowering at us is in fact Detective Noah Corbin Fox.

"I"—he hitches his thumb over his shoulder, his face looking morbidly long—"was just asking the owners about Hunter. They were kind enough to show me the application he filled out just a few days before he passed." His jaw squares out. "And yes, I was going against orders and investigating. I guess I'm not too fond of the rules myself." His eyes hook to mine before he traces out my body with his gaze.

"Oh, no, no, no," I say, caught off guard that I'm still tucked high in his stepbrother's arms.

Everett lands me safely on my feet and takes a deep breath. "It's not what it looks like."

"It's not?" Noah twitches his head at us incredulously. "Of course, it is. The two of you were enjoying one another's company." His voice dips low, and if I didn't know better, I'd say he was struggling with the words. "I guess I'm okay with that."

"You *guess*?" My heart slaps wildly against my chest. "You either are or you aren't." There. I said it. If Noah has any feelings for me whatsoever, this is his moment to speak now or forever hold his peace. Didn't those kisses mean anything to him? Although, to be fair, he could say the same to me.

My phone bleats in my pocket before he can answer, and I quickly scan over it.

"Oh no," I say, looking up at both Noah and Everett. "It's my sister. She says she thinks her garage may have been broken into."

Noah leans in, rife with concern. "Tell her to call the police and get back in her car. Do not go in the house. I'm on my way. Everett, you keep Lottie here until I give you the all clear."

He takes off, and I choke on my next words before taking Everett by the hand and hightailing it to the parking lot.

"Come on, Everett. I don't care what he says. You're taking me to my sister's."

"But Noah—"

"Noah will have to live with it."

Just like I might have to live without him.

15

We find Lainey perched by the open mouth of the garage, the police already there with two squad cars. It's a horrible sight to see your sister's house lit up with blue and red strobing lights in the night.

"*Lainey*," I say, lunging at her with a hug. Everett sped just as fast as Noah did to get here, but Noah still managed to beat us. To be honest, it felt like I was caught up in some testosterone-fueled game as they kept trying to outrun one another. I'm not sure what happened between the two of them, way back when, but this screams unresolved childhood issues.

I spot Noah already deep inside the garage speaking with a member of the sheriff's department.

"Tell me what happened?" I ask my sister as I quickly inventory all of the boxes from my old apartment, a few of which have toppled to the side.

My sister wraps her arms around herself as she turns to look inside. "Well, I came home and the garage door was ajar. I couldn't figure out why, so I figured it must have been that rash of break-ins we've been having."

Everett strides up next to me. "Is anything missing?"

Lainey shrinks a bit in her oversized plaid coat. "I can't tell. I mean, it's all your stuff, Lottie. How would I know if anything was gone?" She threads her arm through mine. "Does anything look as if it's missing to you?"

I take a step inside, and Noah tips his head over at me, the look of grief slightly veiled in his eyes.

"Actually, it looks as if everything is present and accounted for."

"Look at this"—Everett points over to a couple of bricks that are bucking in the driveway and a loose one tossed to the side—"it looks like your door may not have shut properly."

"Oh no." Lainey tips her head back. "I had it open before I left, looking for a bin of books I've been meaning to donate." Lainey is forever donating books to the library. She once told me that working at the library felt as if she were visiting old friends. And she would be, considering half the books are donated from her private collection. "I guess it was a false alarm."

"Not to worry." The sheriff standing next to Noah comes over. "Better safe than sorry. It's an odd thing, but those robberies seemed to have come to a stop abruptly a couple weeks ago. Whoever was doing it has either been caught or killed." He nods our way. "Goodnight, folks. We're heading on out." He takes off, and my mouth falls open as a thought comes to me.

I glance over to the spot Noah was standing in, but he's gone.

The sound of a car purring to life ignites behind us, and I turn just in time to see him taking off with a wave.

Everett huffs at the sight, "Don't take it personally, Lemon. It's me he's ticked off at. I can promise you that." He offers Lainey and me a slight bow. "Enjoy the rest of your night, ladies. I'm glad it was nothing."

We watch as he takes off, and my sister lands her head on my shoulder.

"You really showed up with the cavalry. Have you settled on one yet?"

"Yes, I've settled on one. It's just that he can't seem to settle on me."

"Option B isn't so bad himself. Honestly, there are no wrong choices here."

"There's a wrong choice, all right," I say, turning back around and looking into the cozy little garage—"and that choice would be me."

"Oh, *you*." Lainey is quick to swat me. "So, I guess those garage thieves moved on after all."

"Or died." I can't help but think it's the latter. "I'm starting to wonder if I knew Hunter Fisher at all."

The next few days are maddening with nonstop baking as dozens upon dozens of devil's food cupcakes are frosted in festive Halloween hues of orange, purple, and green, festooned with meringue ghosts, bright blue wizard hats, and licorice spiders.

But my mind is far from the task at hand. I can't help but mull over the case while I pour batter into another batch of cupcake molds. As far as I'm concerned, Bear isn't at all a suspect, but then, I guess I can't really take anyone off the list just yet. Then there's Chuck Popov, who as Bear suggested didn't lend Hunter a dime. Although, Hunter could have borrowed money from Chuck behind Bear's back. And Chuck did seem a little rough around the edges that day when I mentioned Hunter's name. Perhaps he was just a disgruntled colleague? However, if Hunter owed him money, people can get unfriendly real quick when a little cash comes between them. Not that I'm assuming it was a small sum Hunter borrowed. But, as for now, that's just my imagination running wild. Until something solid comes up, Chuck isn't really on my radar. Then there's Mom's new boyfriend, Wallace, who said he tried to get Hunter a loan but failed. That actually penciled out. And interestingly enough, led us to evidence of Hunter's stripper ex-girlfriend, the one with the kid. And, of course, there's Micheline Roycroft. She didn't do it. I'd stake my life on it. Although, she was useful in tipping me off as far as where I could find Stella. Stella. I shake my head. She was so angry. For an ex-girlfriend, she sure as heck didn't so much as shed a tear. Come to think of it, she didn't look too torn up at his funeral either. Stella. Maybe once I recuperate from tonight I'll head back to Girls Unlimited and have another chat with her? I'm sure Everett won't mind one bit escorting me back to that flesh-fest. I roll my eyes at the thought.

Keelie helps me transport the multitude of boxes to the McMurry Pumpkin Patch with just minutes to spare before the Fall-O-Ween Fest gets underway.

The crowds have already descended upon the place with costumes that range from adorable to looking like they outright belong in a horror movie. Keelie and I lean toward the adorable end of the spectrum with Keelie dressed up as a fairy in a pale green tutu and sparkly leotard to go along with it. Her makeup looks as if a fairy herself showed up to apply the magical wonder, but Keelie being Keelie has decided to vamp the look up a bit with some heavy eyeliner for dramatic flair. And have I mentioned that her leotard is low-cut in the front and that tutu hardly covers her rear?

"You're going to freeze to death," I say, shivering myself.

"I told you. I'm determined to find my fae prince who will wrap me in his strong arms and return the feeling to my s-s-skin." Her teeth chatter as she says it. "You're no better yourself."

I glance down at the short blue dress and my tall black boots with their cute crisscross pattern running down the front. That badge on my chest is proudly glinting in the light, and the patches that read *police* over my sleeves look official. Keelie lent me a pair of official handcuffs she swiped from her father, and I'm terrified I'll do something dumb like lock myself in them, so I'm letting them dangle from my belt for now as a flashy accessory.

"I *know*." I shiver. "But I couldn't help it. There's some irony to it. Besides, when Lily said she'd bring in one of her spares for me, I had no idea it would be so suggestive."

"*Please*"—she tips her head back and laughs openly at the thought—"everything that girl does is suggestive."

"Amen to that," I say as a giant mass of humanity fills the pumpkin farm as far as the eye can see. The entire grounds are decorated with scarecrows and skeletons, witches and ghosts. The nonstop screams from the haunted hayrides can be heard for miles despite the fact they have speakers set up and are blaring Halloween-themed music on a loop.

"No, no." Keelie shakes her head at something behind me. "Do not turn around." Her hands grip me by the shoulders. "Say, I really want to try that blue cotton candy. How about we each get one and see who can finish up the fastest?"

"We already know it's going to be me. We do that every year, Keelie," I say, straining to turn around. "What is it that you don't want me to see?" I break free from her hold, and as soon as my eyes snag on a horrible sight, the wind gets knocked right out of me.

"Well then." It comes out with a contrived sense of strength. "I guess we really are over."

Off in the distance, standing in line for the coveted haunted hayrides are Noah and Ivy Fairbanks. Her long, red hair glimmers like copper as she laughs at something he said, and my heart breaks just witnessing the event.

I stagger backward until I end up at the petting zoo and spot a familiar stripper dressed as a scantily clad bunny—far more than she wears most weeknights. She's on her knees helping the little child in her arms pet a baby goat, and I gasp when I see the little boy's face. That dirty blond hair, that olive skin—sure, a lot of people have those physical attributes, but that face looks a little too familiar. I've seen that face a thousand times before, and it wasn't on him. A dark-haired man steps in front of the boy, blocking him from my view, and I glance up to find the man who was comforting Stella at the funeral, the same one who saved me from the scaffolding the day Hunter died.

A crowd moves in between us, and I lose them in the happy chaos of the evening.

Kids shout into the night at the trunk-or-treat lot next to me, and suddenly this entire farm is nothing but a cacophony of sounds.

Just as I'm about to pull out my phone and call Noah, I suddenly remember we're not exactly on speaking terms, and he just might be having the time of his haunted life with Ivy on that spooky hayride.

I glance over and spot the haunted corn maze and frown. That about sums up my life. Everywhere I turn there's a dead end—or a dead pet. And right about now, I'm not crazy about either.

"*Lottie!*" a cheery voice calls out, and it's Molly with Ken trailing by her side. "You did a fantastic job on the cupcakes! You really are a genius in the kitchen."

"And you're far too kind. It was really—" I'm about to segue into an entire litany of self-deprecating thoughts when I spot Micheline Roycroft standing next to Bear, and the two of them seem to be having a heated debate while they each hold one of my genius cupcakes in their hands. I'm betting they're not anywhere near the topic of my IQ. "I'm sorry. I see someone that I need to speak with. I'll be right back."

I speed over just as Bear and Micheline hit a lull in their argument.

"Happy Halloween," I say, looking to the both of them without the aid of a smile. Truth be told, there's not a hint of anything cheery in my voice either. I'm a bit peeved at them at the moment, because it's becoming clear the two of them know more than they're letting on.

"You look great, Lot." Bear frowns while craning his head past me.

Micheline is dressed as a vampire with trails of fake blood running down her chin. She looks past me as well, and I follow her gaze to where Stella and the little boy were just a moment ago.

"That's him, isn't it?" I look back to the two of them accusingly. "Hunter had a son. That's why he had to keep borrowing money." A slap of shock detonates over me all at once as the pieces to the puzzle fall into place. "And the two of you knew about it." I shake my head incredulously. "Why? Why keep it a secret?"

"*Lottie*," Bear moans. "Hunter didn't want anyone to know."

"Why? It's his kid! Hunter loved children. He would have made a great father."

"I agree." Micheline nods, but those wild eyes are saying something else entirely. "But you don't know Stella. She's a nightmare to deal with."

"Was she threatening him?" I step in front of Bear as I demand the answer. "Do you think Stella or that creepy boyfriend of hers did this?"

Bear's face hardens to flint, and he takes off into the crowd without warning.

"*Bear!*" Micheline calls after him. "We're not finished," she shouts before threading through a thicket of people, and she too is gone before I can stop her.

"Oh my God," I whisper as I pull out my phone once again. A part of me demands I call Jack, Keelie's father, the captain of the Ashford Sheriff's Department, but my fingers find another name, and I put in a call to that number instead. But Noah doesn't pick up. I bolt into the crowd in the same direction Bear and Micheline took off in and run for what feels like half a mile before I head away from the crowd to catch my breath. From the corner of my eye, I spot a dark-haired man looking at me just as he ducks into the haunted corn maze, and hot on his heels are Stella and that sweet baby who bears a striking resemblance to his father.

My heart drums up my throat as I head on over.

Corn Maze, I hit send before I realize I sent it to Noah and not Bear.

But I don't waste time rectifying the error. Instead, I head over to the haunted corn maze myself and step on in.

It's time to confront the mother of Hunter's child, and maybe his killer as well.

16

There have been moments in my life that I've been morbidly afraid, frightened out of my mind for far lesser reasons. But at this moment, entering into a dimly lit maze—haunted at that—I'm riding the zenith of terror. I'm so far outside of my mind with fright it almost feels sublime.

The corn maze is a walled-in wonder filled with erroneous twists and turns—and don't forget a horror around each corner. I should know, I've been once before—ironically while I was dating Bear. I screamed until my vocal cords went out and finally closed my eyes and made Bear get us the heck out of there. I swore I would never subject myself to the terror ever again and, yet, here I am.

My feet move brazenly at a quickened clip in hopes of catching up to Stella and her man.

The sound of a child crying can be heard at a distance, and my pace picks up. No sooner do I round the next corner than a zombie-looking creature jumps out at me with a tiny zombie baby doll in her arms, and I snatch it from her without thinking.

"Hey, lady"—the zombie woman calls after me as I take off—"where you going? That's a part of my bit! Ah, geez."

Her voice fades to nothing as I bullet past vampires jumping out of caskets, monsters and maniacs, werewolves and space aliens. I pass a small crowd of teenagers who scream their heads off as I bolt past them with the zombie baby still in my hands, but I'm a woman on a mission, and I'm not stopping until I get the truth out of Stella.

The violent sound of a power tool grows in ferocity as I propel myself from one dead end to the other, and I pause, holding onto my knees, panting so hard I start to feel light-headed. The glint of something small and furry wraps around my ankle, and a shrill scream unleashes from me as I try my best to stomp the life out of the creature. But the tiny beast only lifts its cute little face at me and appears to chatter out a laugh.

I suck in a quick breath as I bend over and give the ghostly little cutie a scratch over his back.

"You scared the living daylights out of me." Another breath hitches in my throat as an idea comes to me. "Take me to Hunter's killer! I've got an entire fleet of deputies I can employ to wrangle them to justice. Wouldn't you love that?"

Its bushy little tails whips back and forth, and it takes off without so much as a wink.

"Here goes nothing," I say as I follow along after it.

It leads the way straight to a split in the road, and for the life of me I can't tell which direction the sound of that buzz saw is coming from.

"Just FYI," I whisper to it. "I'm practically allergic to spooks. If at all possible, I'd like to avoid anyone who's even remotely near a chainsaw."

The tiny fuzzy creature chirps up at me, and I'd swear I was just laughed at by dead vermin. It leads to the right where the maze opens up to a clearing, and I spot a couple with a baby up ahead.

"Good job, little guy," I pant as I do my best to blend in with corn stalks.

Stella turns and spots me before pulling her boyfriend to the left, and just as I'm about to follow, they come right back to where they started.

"Dead end?" I can't help but chide them.

The poor baby has his head tucked into his mother's neck, too afraid to look at his surroundings, and I don't blame him. Stella looks on fire as if she thrived on the adrenaline, but her boyfriend has a stiffness about him as if he were trying his best to get them out of this situation at any cost. And that's what I have to fear the most.

Bear must be on my trail by now. Both he and Micheline were after them. They'll be here soon. I have to believe it. I step forward, and they back their way into another offshoot as it opens up to a large octagon-shaped space that's—

Out jumps a man in a hockey mask wielding that horrifically loud chainsaw, and the three of us howl in unison.

Stella and her boyfriend hightail it to the back of the octagon, entrapping themselves with nowhere to go. Instinctually, I block the exit, holding my hands out like a goaltender with the zombie baby dangling from my wrist.

"That's Hunter's baby boy. Isn't it, Stella?" I shout up over the roar of the motor. The man in the hockey mask does his best to jump and jive while wielding his weapon, but not one of us pays him any mind.

"What do you care?" she shouts back, cradling the back of the baby's head protectively. "This isn't any of your business. But you've been putting yourself where you don't belong right from the beginning." She jerks her head toward her boyfriend. "Get me out of here, Jonas."

The man with the chainsaw growls and shakes his weapon but to no avail. He got the reaction he wanted out of us the first time, and now we're onto something far more frightening—ourselves.

"*Jonas—*" I call out, and he looks up at me with a steady gaze as if he were calculating how to burst right through me, and then a thought occurs to me. "Oh my God." I straighten as I come to an epiphany. "You rigged the scaffolding, didn't you?"

He looks to Stella, and they exchange a steely glance.

"You wanted Hunter out of the picture—but why? You had Stella. Hunter didn't."

Stella lets out a riotous groan, and the man with the chainsaw tosses a hand in the air in exasperation.

"Aw, come on," the masked man growls. "I'm supposed to be the scary one here," he whines, and yet we continue to dismiss him.

Stella takes a few brazen steps my way. "He didn't have a problem with Hunter. *I* did." The baby in her arms whimpers, and she takes a moment to soothe him. "Hunter was supposed to give me enough money to live off, and instead, I was stuck at that dive bar dancing for dollars. You think I wanted to twirl around that pole all night? But Hunter didn't care. All he wanted was to take my son away from me. He wanted him. He was trying to steal him away."

I shake my head in disbelief. "I'm his good friend, and I didn't even know he had a kid. That can't be true," I howl over the whirl of the chainsaw.

Jonas snatches her by the elbow a moment. "I told you he wasn't out to get you. You're paranoid, and you have been ever since you had the baby."

"*Enough!*" Stella raises her foot and shoves it into his stomach before whipping past me and out of sight.

I'm about to dash after her when my feet are knocked out from underneath me. The zombie doll goes flying, and my hands slap down over the ground before I inadvertently kiss damp Honey Hollow soil. I scamper to my knees as Jonas tries to leap over me, and I reach up and grab ahold of the bottom of his jeans.

Jonas falls to the side, knocking down the man in the hockey mask with him. The chainsaw bounces wildly behind them as I scramble to my feet.

And just as I'm about to hightail it out of there, Jonas snatches up the roaring weapon and jabs it my way.

"Don't move!" he shouts at the top of his lungs, and every cell in my body is suddenly immobilized. "This isn't about you. Leave us alone. Stella needs help. She's been a different person ever since she had the kid."

"You've been with her as long as she's been with Hunter? I don't get it. How did that not strain your relationship? You must really love your girlfriend."

"*Girlfriend*?" His head ticks back as if I threw him for a loop. "Stella's not my girlfriend. She's my sister. I'm trying to get her the help she needs."

It's as if time stands still, and this entire night turns on its ear once again.

"You're trying to help her. She's not well." I shake my head. "You didn't kill Hunter, did you?"

The man in the hockey mask takes a swipe at Jonas, and he swings the weapon the man's direction. A part of me says run—and another far more logical part says he can outrun me even with a chainsaw in his hands.

I snatch the zombie doll off the ground and toss it in the air at him, and he slices its head off without hesitation. The man with the hockey mask knocks the chainsaw out of his hand and wrestles him to the ground. As much as my feet are twitching to bolt, those handcuffs Keelie gifted me catch the light, and an idea springs to life. Perhaps not a good one—in fact, one that can backfire spectacularly, but I pluck the handcuffs free and fall to my knees.

"What the hell are you doing, lady?" A muffled cry comes from our masked friend.

"This is a citizen's arrest!" I bark over the roar of the motor. Jonas continues to struggle, but he's effectively pinned to the ground. It takes two tries to leash his left wrist with the cuff. "Get his hands together!" I scream at the masked man, but Jonas is working hard to overpower him, and I don't have another moment to think about it. Instead, I cuff his wrist to the man in the mask and run like hell.

The maze goes on forever, spookier, darker, and with no sign of that useless squirrel. Instead, I wise up and follow a couple of screaming teenagers right out the exit. My feet stumble to a halt as I pant into the night while surveying the landscape.

To my right sits the open pumpkin field, to my left a midway with games and an entire legion of large round barrels filled with water. Apples bob lightly along the surface as they wait patiently for the nighttime festivities to fully commence. The apple bobbing competition is the one that crowns the night. It's a long-standing tradition that the McMurrys enjoy right along with their patrons.

A glowing beam of light twitches near the base of those apple barrels, and I can't help but give a weak smile as I spot my furry friend. It seems to tick its head for me to follow it as it scampers over to a mob of people in the thick of the midway and, low and behold, leaning on a post, I spot a head of long, dark hair, that curvy body. The sequin of her bodysuit gives her away like a disco ball spraying out a spasm of light in our dimly lit world.

Every muscle in my body propels me in that direction, and before Stella can bolt I'm on her. The child isn't anywhere in sight, and my heart thumps wildly, almost afraid to see what she's done.

Stella makes a run toward the barrels, and I'm right on her tail.

"You killed Hunter!" I scream up over the music, incensed that she had gotten away with it for so long.

Stella stops cold next to a barrel, her wild pants pumping from her in long, white plumes.

"He wanted to take Travis away from me. I was just some disgusting breeding factory to him."

"Not true. Hunter would never look at another human being that way. Especially not the mother of his child."

"He looked at me that way." A dark laugh strums from her as her eyes glisten like shards. Stella looks every bit like a woman unmoored. "He thought I was trash because of what I did for a living. Sure, it was great when he first met me, but once I had the baby, he didn't think I was fit enough to raise it."

"Is that why he needed so much money? He was giving it all to you?" I ask as I continue to cautiously inch my way toward her.

"*Ha!*" she belts it out into the night. "He wasn't giving it all to me. He was giving it to a fancy lawyer in Ashford. He was trying to get full custody. He wanted me permanently out of the picture. I had to take things into my own hands and make sure it was him who never got to raise our son."

My gut wrenches just hearing it. "You didn't want to shoot him, did you?"

A high-pitched laugh escapes her. "No, I didn't. I wanted to smash his skull in!" she riots into my face. "I went to that site he was working on early that morning. Sun wasn't even up. I hauled those bags of concrete mix up that scaffolding myself. My damn brother wouldn't help me." Her gaze disappears past me. "I had to do everything myself."

"They must have weighed seventy pounds apiece." And there were three.

She glowers over at me. "You'd be surprised what a mother would do for her son. It gives you supernatural strength just when you need it most."

"I can imagine." I come in so close I can reach out and touch her. "They'll go easy on you," I whisper. "Jonas said you've been having trouble since you've had the baby. I'm sure they'll give you a top-notch psychologist who can help you out."

Her eyes widen to the size of twin moons. "I'm not going to prison. I've killed once, and I'm not afraid to do it again." She glances to my neck a moment. "If I had a gun, I'd kill you. I'm sorry this won't be as quick."

In the blink of an eye my entire head is submerged beneath the water as she struggles to hold me under. I buck and seize as I wriggle my way back to the surface, catching an enormous breath as soon as I hit air.

Stella digs her knee into the back of mine, and I collapse toward the barrel once again. "You little bitch," she roars as she dunks me under so fast so hard it feels as if she has a bionic grip over me. Stella is right. She's got supernatural strength right when she needs it most. But so do I.

My elbow flies back into her gut, and she doubles over, loosening her hold over me long enough for me to rise back out, gasping and sputtering.

Stella yanks me back by the hair and tries to throw a punch at me, but I duck right out of her line of fire.

"Freeze! Hands up!" a voice thunders from behind, but Stella doesn't bother with protocol. Instead, she growls like a lioness, and I'm right back in that water, her body pressed over mine, heavy as if a building were lying over me.

The pressure releases, and I cork to the surface, only to find Stella being plucked off of me by none other than Noah Fox.

"No—" I struggle to say his name as the entire vicinity fills with men in uniform. Noah hands Stella off to the sheriffs before speeding my way.

"*Lottie.*" He runs his lips over mine, holding me tight as my arms collapse over him. "Are you all right? I need to get you to the hospital—make sure she didn't hurt you."

"I'm all right," I pant as if I just ran the circumference of the planet. "She didn't hurt me. I promise I'm fine." I cling to Noah as if he were a life raft, and he is. "Stella killed Hunter. She confessed to the whole thing. Where's the baby? Where's Hunter's son?" I struggle to crane my neck past him. I'm so exhausted I can hardly hold myself up.

"He's fine." Noah brushes his thumbs over my cheeks. "She handed him off to Micheline just a little while ago. Bear told me." Noah searches my features with his eyes as if it were the first time he was seeing me. "All that matters to me is you, Lottie. You're all I care about. You came into my life and upturned everything I thought I knew. All of those things I swore I'd never feel again, those things that I forbid myself from feeling—you didn't give me any damn choice. I'm yours, Lottie Kenzie Lemon, and every day without you is miserable. I need you in my life. I need you by my side. I've fallen hard for you, Lottie. Please tell me that you feel the same or I'll go insane."

A laugh bubbles from my throat as I bear hard into his pine green eyes. "*Yes.* I do feel the same." The world around us feels as if it slows down, as if all of time stands still just for the two of us. "I'm falling for you, Noah—and, I'm afraid." My affect falls flat as I spill that singular truth that I wish never crested my lips.

A pained smile expands across his gorgeous face. "Don't be. We're in this together. Through thick and thin."

"I'm pretty sure we've seen our fair share of thick." I bite down over my bottom lip. "Or is it thin that we've seen? Sorry, my head's a bit fuzzy." I tuck a wet lock of hair behind my ear.

Noah tips his head back, those glowing green eyes never leaving mine. "I don't know if it's thick or thin, but I do know one thing for sure. I'm never letting anything petty get between us ever again. Everett called the other night and let me know that the two of you were just friends. He says he's happy for me, for us. He doesn't want me to screw it up."

I cock my head playfully. "Neither do I."

"That makes three of us." His dimples ignite as he bows in for a kiss. Noah crashes his lips to mine, and we declare exactly how we feel for one another in front of every ghost and goblin, every vampire and werewolf Honey Hollow has to offer.

Noah blesses me with soft pecking kisses before pulling back to get a better look at me. His eyes ride down over my costume, and he growls with approval.

"I fully authorize you to conduct a pat-down any and every time you feel like it, Officer Lemon."

A naughty grin twitches over my lips. "Don't you worry, Detective Fox. I plan on conducting a thorough investigation of your person. I promise to leave no stone unturned." My hand glides over his chest like a threat. "I suggest you obey my authority and get those lips back to mine right this minute."

A dark laugh rumbles in his chest. "Yes, ma'am."

And he does as he's told.

17

Halloween in Honey Hollow has always been filled with its fair share of terrors, but on that night, there was also a genuine relief that Hunter Fisher's killer had finally been brought to justice. Stella was arrested and is currently awaiting trial. Jonas was booked as an accomplice, and Everett said that although he was a party to aiding and abetting a murderer, that because of the circumstances the legal system wouldn't go tough on him. Stella is getting the help she needs for her paranoia, and it was brought to light that a part of that paranoia was actually triggered from the birth itself. Baby Travis is with Bear's mother, and no one is more delighted to have an infant in her care than she is. In fact, in light of the new circumstances, we've decided to host a celebration of life party for Hunter, and I insisted on hosting it at the bakery. Keelie had the chefs prepare sandwiches while I baked an entire litany of every dessert I know that Hunter loved—and he loved them all.

The crowd is small, but the atmosphere is cheery.

The surprise Nell and Keelie had been hinting at ever since the grand opening arrived last night just in time for the celebration, and Bear and his crew worked well into the early hours of the morning to install it. When I arrived, they were just leaving, and I about had a heart attack seeing them here. Bear was the one who got to show it to me—and as soon as he flipped the switch, my heart burst like a piñata filled with love. It's an extension of that glorious oak tree staking claim in the middle of the honey pot with its branches elongating like tendrils all throughout the café portion of the Cutie Pie Bakery and Cakery. I called both Keelie and Nell and cried over the phone as I thanked them. Each branch is carefully entwined with twinkle lights, and it adds a flair of magic to this already enchanted piece of Honey Hollow.

Noah holds me by the waist as Bear heads our way.

"You've got a keeper," he scowls at Noah. "And you'd better keep her, because if you ever let her go, I'm taking her back." He winks my way.

"You're hilarious." I can't help but tease him. I've made it more than clear to Bear that the door to any intimate relationship between us is forever closed. "So tell us, Bear"—I pause to glance to Noah who offers a confirming nod—"was it Hunter that was behind all of those garage robberies?"

Bear takes a breath and sweeps his eyes over the vicinity. "All right. I found a bunch of crap in his truck one day, and he may have implicated himself." He closes his eyes, his entire body sagging with remorse. "He was pawning stuff and giving the money to Stella. She kept threatening to leave with the kid, and she had Hunter where she wanted him. The poor guy didn't see a way out."

Noah groans, "So, he was never trying to sue for full custody?"

"Nope." Bear gives a wistful shake of the head. "In fact, I was the one who threatened her with it. And that's exactly why I was so angry with myself when I saw him lying there in the alley. I had my suspicions it might have been her or someone connected to her."

I gasp at the revelation. "Bear! You should have turned her in. We could have avoided this entire mess."

"I know, I know. But Hunter made me swear on his mother's grave that I wouldn't do a thing to cause trouble in her life no matter what happened. I think he knew he was staring down the barrel of a gun. And, in the end, he did just that." Bear drops his gaze to the floor before slapping the back of his neck, something he usually does when he's trying to hide his emotions. "Excuse me. I think I need to step outside for a minute."

"Don't be too hard on yourself," I say, catching him by the wrist. "Hunter would never want that. And neither do I."

A soft moment bounces between us like a truce, and Bear gives a sheepish smile before heading out the door.

Nell steps over, her silver hair catching the twinkle lights from above and it gives her the ethereal glow of an angel.

"Well done, my dear." She cups my cheeks with her sweet wrinkled fingers and presses a kiss to my cheek. "Now when my time comes, don't you dare let them host one of those depressing tearjerkers down in the church's rec room. I fully expect the entire lot of you to celebrate my life."

I shudder against Noah at the thought. "Nell! Don't talk like that. You're miles away from going anywhere." She may not be, but it certainly felt like the right thing to say. "Besides, I need you." I look right into her crystal blue eyes when I say it, and they swell with tears in an instant. "Thank you again for this beautiful work of art." I glance up to the glowing branches above us. "It makes me feel like a princess every time I see it. It also makes me feel like family."

"Oh, Lottie, you are a princess." She offers my cheek a hearty pinch. "And I certainly love you as my own family." Her mouth remains open as if she were about to add something to it, but she lets out a sigh instead. "I'm afraid I'm through for the night. Each time you look at those branches, I want you to know that you are a part of my family tree." There's a pained look in her eyes, and I can't quite pinpoint why. Most likely because she feels sorry for me, for the way my journey in this life began on that cold cement floor of the firehouse. "Thank you for having me." She brushes another precious kiss to my cheek before threading her way back toward the Honey Pot.

I turn to Noah. "That was a little strange. Didn't you think so?"

But before he can say anything, Keelie bounds over with Lainey, and the two of them pull me in for a quick embrace, temporarily breaking the hold Noah has on me.

Lainey wags a finger in my face. "You are not allowed to scare us like that again. No more running toward danger."

Keelie leans in. "And no more dead bodies," she whispers. "It's not a good look on you. I'm just saying."

The four of us share a morbid laugh as Everett heads in this direction. I can't help but note Collette Jenner scuttling alongside him like a parasite he can't quite get rid of. Okay, so parasite is a bit harsh, but I've scanned my entire lexicon, and that's the best fit I could come up with on such short notice.

Collette rolls her eyes. "I will admit, those cupcakes at the Fall-O-Ween Fest were to die for. I must have eaten ten if I didn't eat thirty."

"Thank you." I'm taken aback by her kind words, and suddenly she's looking less parasite and a bit more human.

Lainey leans in. "Molly said every last one of them disappeared before eight o'clock."

Keelie bounces the curls off her shoulder. "In fact, they were so well sought-after that the calls have been pouring into the Cutie Pie for more large orders."

"They have," I affirm as I look back to Collette. "Say, don't you work for Endeavor PR?"

Her head ticks back a notch. "Everyone knows I work for the best PR company in the country." She smirks up at Everett. "I only go after the best in life."

I clear my throat as she tries to dive her mouth over his. "Anyway, they called this morning and asked if I'd cater the desserts for an awards ceremony they're having next week at the Evergreen Manor."

"VIP awards," she corrects. "And yes, Everett and I will be there with bells on. He's already promised to be my official plus one." She offers a strangulating hug to his arm, but Everett seems unmoved by her psychotic advances. "Oh, and, by the way, my boss is into pumpkin spice everything. Make it worth his while. You don't want to see him unhappy."

"Duly noted and I guess I'll see you there."

Everett gives an approving nod my way. "Everything looks great tonight. You did good, Lemon."

Lainey jumps beside me. "My sister always does good."

Noah tucks a kiss to my cheek. "That she does." He picks up my hand and gives it a squeeze. "I've got some good news for you." Noah sheds that signature cocky grin, and my stomach bisects with heat. "You got the rental house. My realtor called and said you can pick up the keys as soon as you're ready."

"I got the house!" I shout so loud the room breaks out into a cheer right along with me. I'm so excited, I wrap my entire body around Noah's as he spins me gently, and I'm dizzy with happiness, dizzy from the way he makes me feel.

He lands me back on my feet, and both Keelie and Lainey slap me five.

Collette snickers. "That's just dandy. It looks as if Lottie is off the market." She bats her lashes up at Everett. "I'm ready to get off the market myself, big boy. You got any idea of who can fit the bill?" Collette gives his tie a light tug, and it's all I can do not to groan in disapproval.

"No"—he gently removes her hand from his tie—"I don't." He sheds his killer grin—it's such a rare sighting that every girl in the room pauses to observe it. "But I do have some good news of my own that you might like." He winks her way before turning his attention to Noah and me. "I'm moving myself. It looks like I'm heading to Honey Hollow."

"*What*?" both Collette and I cry in unison.

"That's right. Being here reminded me of how much I hate living in the city. And I happened to get a great deal on a house myself. I paid cash in full, and they didn't argue. It's mine now. I'm a full-fledged homeowner."

"Congratulations!" we all shout at the top of our lungs.

The whooping dies down, and Noah gives his stepbrother a handshake. "So, where exactly will you be? I need to know what street to avoid." A grin spreads wide over his face as we laugh it off.

"Country Cottage Road."

"What?" Noah balks. "Really? I don't remember seeing a house for sale in the neighborhood."

"It wasn't. I liked the blue house we toured that day, and when Lottie didn't want it, I made my move. Let's just say the old owners were more than happy with how things worked out."

"We're going to be neighbors!" I give Everett a spontaneous hug and note that Noah is slower to congratulate him this time.

"Great." Noah's head bobs with an unconvincing nod. "Just great."

"It will be great." Everett tips his head back as the two of them stare one another down for a moment.

"It will be very great," I say, pulling Noah in close. "We're all turning a new leaf."

Collette wraps herself around Everett like a suckerfish. "To *new leaves*!"

"To new leaves," we chant back.

Things will undoubtedly be different with our new living arrangements, but I'm determined to make it work. After all, I couldn't imagine my life without either of them in it.

A gray ball of fur hops up onto the brownie tray, and I gasp as my entire body solidifies.

Noah leans in. "Everything okay?"

"Everything is just fine." My head turns toward him, but my eyes never stray from that bushy-tailed visitor.

Everett steps over and points down to the brownie bar as if acknowledging what I see, and I give a little nod. He doesn't hesitate picking up a dark fudge brownie and holding it over his open palm against the table. The tiny woodland spectral hops right over and does its best to nibble. I can't help but coo at the sight and offer an approving nod as Everett and I share a warm smile.

The party dwindles down, and Noah helps me close up shop long after everyone has gone home.

He pulls me into his strong arms as we step outside into the brisk autumn night and looks lovingly into my eyes. "It's official. I belong to you." He tucks a kiss to the nape of my neck. "We're official," he says, swaying back to get a better look at me.

"We're official?"

"That's right. I hope it doesn't sound weird for you to call me your boyfriend. I already called my stepbrother and told him all about my new girlfriend."

"You did? Will I like her when I meet her?" I can't help but tease him, and we share a warm laugh.

"You can't help but love her." His features smooth out as he says the L word, and my heart drums wildly right into my ears.

"You really called Everett?"

He nods, affirming the fact.

"You're a sneak. I love that." There's that L word again, and I suppose it means something even minutely that we both used it back to back. *Love*. That word circles my mind. It begs to be redirected toward him, but I'm afraid I'll scare him off if I do. And just like that, I shake the thought right out of my head. "You know what? I think I—"

Noah gently muzzles me with a lingering, sugar sweet kiss before pulling back with sleepy eyes.

"I want to say it first," he whispers right over my lips. "I need you to hear me say it. I want it to sink into your bones." He pulls back and gazes tenderly into my eyes. "I think I love you, Lottie Lemon. In fact, I know I do."

My lips part as I try my hardest to memorize this moment. "I love you, too, Noah. I do."

The moon shines a spotlight over us as if it were the final scene in some romantic black and white movie. But it's not the final scene for Noah and me. The two of us have just begun.

That crooked grin begins to bloom on his face once again, his eyes never leaving mine.

Noah gently tucks a stray lock behind my ear. "I have a feeling I've just entered into the best season of my life. And I predict that with you by my side every season thereafter will be better and better."

"They never stop getting better?" I bite down over a smile.

"With you in my life, that would be impossible. We're a team, Lottie. And we're building a solid foundation. No pretense, no secrets—filled with honesty and communication."

Noah lands his oven-hot mouth over mine, and we indulge in something richer, far more decadent and sweeter than anything I could whip up in the kitchen. Noah and I are building a solid foundation. No pretense, no secrets—

filled with honesty and communication. But deep down, I know for a fact there is plenty of pretense involved. I am rife with secrets. I am not filled with honesty, not entirely—especially when it comes to my supernatural tendencies. And I will most certainly not communicate a single word about them. It's bad enough I've spilled the supernatural beans to Everett.

No, Noah Fox can never be apprised of that paranormal part of my life.

And because of this, there will always be a thorny secret nestled between us, creating a barrier, a buffer that will forever stand between us.

It's a division, and everyone knows a house divided cannot stand.

But Noah and I are different.

Aren't we?

And I wonder.

A Note from the Author

Join Lottie Lemon and the fine people of Honey Hollow in the next book, PUMPKIN SPICE SACRIFICE (MURDER IN THE MIX 3)!

Acknowledgements

Thank you to YOU, the reader, for delving into the MURDER IN THE MIX world with me. I hope you love Lottie and Honey Hollow as much as I do! I hope you'll join me on the next leg of the MURDER IN THE MIX adventure for more mayhem and mischief!

A special thank you to Jodie Tarleton for your extraordinary vision. You are amazing and a wonderful support. There are just no words to convey how thankful I am for you.

A HUGE thank you to the amazing Kaila Eileen Turingan-Ramos. Is there anything you can't do? I am in awe of your superpowers.

A mighty big thank you to Shay Rivera, beta extraordinaire! Your ongoing support and encouragement are well appreciated! Your future is so bright, I have no doubt you will move mountains.

Sister hugs to Lisa Markson. You're amazing and I love you. Thank you for being a friend.

To the beautiful Paige Maroney Smith, there is no one like you. Thank you is such a small sentiment when compared to how grateful I really am to know you. Love you, girl!

And last, but never least, thank you to Him who sits on the throne. Worthy is the Lamb! Glory and honor and power are yours. I owe you everything.

About the Author

Addison Moore is a **New York Times**, **USA Today**, and **Wall Street Journal** bestselling author who writes contemporary and paranormal romance. Her work has been featured in **Cosmopolitan** Magazine. Previously she worked as a therapist on a locked psychiatric unit for nearly a decade. She resides on the West Coast with her husband, four wonderful children, and two dogs where she eats too much chocolate and stays up way too late. When she's not writing, she's reading.

Feel free to visit her at:

Website: www.addisonmoore.com
Facebook: Addison Moore Author
Twitter: @AddisonMoore
Instagram: @AuthorAddisonMoore
http://addisonmoorewrites.blogspot.com

Made in the USA
Las Vegas, NV
05 July 2021